DISTURBING THE RING OF FIRE

WOLF BLASER JR.

ARCHWAY
PUBLISHING

Archway Publishing books may be ordered through booksellers or by contacting:

Archway Publishing
1663 Liberty Drive
Bloomington, IN 47403
www.archwaypublishing.com
1 (888) 242-5904

ISBN: 978-1-4808-7397-1 (sc)
ISBN: 978-1-4808-7396-4 (e)

Library of Congress Control Number: 2019931292

Print information available on the last page.

Archway Publishing rev. date: 01/16/2019

Contents

Chapter 1

Department of State in South Korea

The Ring of Fire is a large series of underground geological shelves that have caused earthquakes and tsunamis over the years in Southeast Asia.

Tom Vance became aware of the Ring of Fire while attending a geology class in high school. It was in high school that Tom found out how much he enjoyed geology and that he wanted to have a career in the field. Tom was a tall man, standing six five and weighing over three hundred pounds. He had brown eyes and blond hair although he had lost much of his hair over the years. Tom spent four years at Stanford where he earned a degree in geology. After college, he took a job with the US State Department. With his expertise, he was assigned to the US Embassy in Seoul, South Korea. He headed the department that monitored the underground plates that made up the Ring of Fire. His position in the State Department had just been created in the past year.

He wasn't alone in his job; he had an assistant to oversee a group of thirty people. Some of them were geologists, and some were support personnel. One of the geologists was Rachel Collins. She was a petite woman with dark-black hair and brown eyes. She was from South Korea and had attended school in the United States. Rachel's parents had lived in the United States for many years before moving back to Seoul. This was the main reason they had given her an American name. She had moved back to South Korea after she graduated from the University of Southern California. Rachel was Tom's right-hand person.

They spent many days traveling to countries around South Korea, such as Japan, Indonesia, and the Philippines. In these countries, they had set up an extensive network of earthquake-monitoring devices. Some of the devices were located close to the ocean, and some of the devices were located up in the mountains. If there was an active volcano, they would certainly make sure an earthquake device was in place. Tom was very precise in the way he planned the trips to the monitoring stations. In his mind, he would calculate the time it would take to check each station. When they were ready to travel to a station, he would create a detailed list of items to check, and he'd put a box next to each item so items could be checked off as they were completed.

Like most people, when they traveled to these other countries, they would always stay in the same hotels and eat at the same restaurants. "Who's going to pick where we eat tonight, Rachel?" Tom said while pulling a coin from his pocket. "Heads you pick the restaurant, tails I pick." Tom flipped the coin and it landed on heads. "Gosh, you've won this coin toss at least four times now," Tom said.

"I'm just lucky, Tom," replied Rachel. "Tonight we're going to eat at the Japanese restaurant downtown."

"That's not too bad. I like that restaurant also," Tom replied. "I'm getting better at using chopsticks!"

"I'm happy that you are able to use chopsticks. Nothing says foreigner more than an inability to use chopsticks," she said.

Before going to bed at a hotel, Tom always set the alarm on his phone. He never liked the wakeup call from the hotel. The sound of the hotel phone ringing startled him. His phone alarm ring tone was more peaceful.

Each monitoring station was set up the same, with the satellite communications that would constantly send data to the main office in Seoul along with GPS coordinates and the name of the station. The hard data that was sent continuously consisted of the seismic information at different elevations in the ground. If there was some movement below or above in the plates, this information would consist of the depth of the disturbance and the strength of the movement. Because there were no cell towers in these remote areas, there was no phone system that could be used at the site.

The monitoring sites located near active volcanoes were of interest to Tom. There was more activity around these areas, typically small seismic events. The events were small enough in size that they posed no problems to the surrounding villages or cities. The last time there was an event that affected these areas had taken place many years ago. There were five volcanic sites Tom had listed around the Ring of Fire.

On his list were the Mayon volcano located in Albay, Philippines; Mount Bromo located in East Java, Indonesia; Mount Hallasan in South Korea; Mount Aso in Japan; and Mount Pinatubo in the Philippines.

"Pick up the pace, old man. I think I've aged a year since we started this hike to the station," Rachel said.

"Hey, cut me some slack. I'm five years older than you are," Tom replied. "Besides I've been wearing myself out using this machete to clear the path to the monitor. Not to mention stopping to swipe away a fly that wants to bother me," he added.

"How much longer until we reach the station?" Rachel said.

"Only another half mile of hiking. I'm going to need to change my shirt because I'm completely wet from sweat," Tom said.

"Good thing I'm not standing next to you because you probably need more deodorant also," she said.

Arriving at the station, Tom pulled out his laptop computer and inserted the cable that connected the computer to the monitor. "We need to perform our routine check on the monitor," Tom said.

"I'll check that the solar panel is charging the station, and I'll check to see if the signal between the station and the office in Seoul is active and strong," said Rachel.

"I'll finish the check on the computer to make sure the signal strength is strong and penetrating the ground. It needs to be one and five to detect most seismic events," he said. Each number represented a thousand feet, so the range was from one thousand to five thousand feet in the ground. They would try to have the necessary materials on hand in case they needed to fix something on the station. Sometimes they did not have the part they needed and would order it then make a second trip to repair the station. They needed to make sure the equipment was in good shape, even though, if something were to break down, a signal would be sent to the main office. It was better to provide preventative maintenance on the stations than to wait for one of them to break down. These stations needed to be running twenty-four seven to ensure early detection of any activity.

Along with all the earthquake-monitoring stations were tsunami-warning stations located in the ocean. An earthquake under the ocean would shake the water and potentially cause large waves. This had occurred several times over the years. Some of the waves had been so tall they had come inland and destroyed buildings and caused loss of life.

There were monitors in the Pacific Ocean several miles from land, but many places along the shores lacked sirens. If there was an earthquake that resulted in a tsunami, sirens were critical because they gave people extra minutes to move away from the beaches and seek higher ground. There were some sirens in larger cities along the shores of the oceans, but not enough. These monitors were tied to the main office in Seoul through a satellite system.

Performing preventative maintenance on these monitors was more difficult than working on land-based monitors. They had to take a boat out into the ocean to reach each monitor. Once they reached the monitor, a small crane on the boat would hold the monitor close to the boat for inspection and possible repair. The ocean buoy monitors were reliable, and rarely broke down.

Tom recalled one trip they had been on to check on the tsunami monitor. The boat had stopped running many miles from shore, leaving Tom and Rachel stranded until nighttime because there was a problem having another boat come out to tow the disabled boat in. The problem turned out to be a leak in the fuel line that caused them to run out of gas. They rescheduled the maintenance check for another day. He still laughed about this incident because something like that rarely happened.

With all the monitors to physically check, it would take Tom and Rachel several months to perform the work, but Tom sent additional teams out to visit the sites so that every monitor would be checked once a year. Included in this time, for Tom only, was a mandatory two-week trip back to Washington DC every year for meetings. Rachel would remain in Seoul while he was gone.

The meetings Tom attended in Washington with his superiors at the State Department were specifically related to the Ring of Fire and the monitoring of potential earthquakes and tsunamis. There was usually a total of five people in the meetings, including Tom. The other four were his superiors. There was only one out of the four that Tom would speak to and report to when he was in Seoul. His name was Kyle Wright. The other three were higher up the chain in the State Department; one of them was the main person in charge of Asia.

When Tom was in Washington, he would always make a trip to his favorite Italian restaurant. There were Italian restaurants in South Korea, but nothing that compared to the restaurant in DC. Over the years, he had been to most of the monuments in Washington, so he did not revisit them. The meetings that took place during the two weeks tied him up for most of the time.

Tom was not a political person, but he understood that his visit was required yearly. He did not like the politics that were associated with this city and his superiors. This was the only time during the year that he wore a suit and tie. The rest of the year, he wore jeans and short-sleeved shirts. During his meetings, he kept his conversation to a minimum, discussing only the facts and leaving out speculation and guessing. If asked if he thought there might be an earthquake in the future, he would answer only with the facts generated by the computer and would not speculate.

The worst thing Tom experienced during these trips was the long plane flight from Seoul to Washington. He was working for the government, so of course he had to fly coach. His size made the trip uncomfortable. He had tried, but sleeping on the plane was not a possibility for him. For him, the trip to Washington was more irritating than the plane trip back to Seoul. At least the plane trip back would mean he would soon be sleeping in his own bed.

His home in Seoul was located approximately twenty-five minutes from the airport and thirty minutes from his office. Tom's home was a two-bedroom house with a single garage. He owned a Ford pickup truck and used the truck to drive around Seoul. He was a good cook, so he did not eat out much. Sometimes during his yearly two-week vacations, he would load up his truck and drive around South Korea.

When he was at work in Seoul, he was given a State Department vehicle to drive to the active volcanos in South Korea. For other trips to volcanoes and monitoring sites, he rented a vehicle. Tom had a company credit card, so he could rent hotels and pay for food.

The beginning of March brought a normal day at the office for Tom. In the morning, he had a meeting with several of the staff members to discuss potential locations for new monitors. While they were in the meeting, the audible alarm sounded in the main monitoring room. The sound was similar to a fire alarm, and its purpose was to alert anyone in the office of a seismic event. "What is going on?" Tom said. He quickly got up and exited the meeting to look at monitors in the main control room to see what had been detected. "Oh no!" he said. "This is a significant event."

Rachel was standing next to him, "I hope there are no casualties," she said. The monitors detected an earthquake off the coast of Japan. The size of the earthquake was enormous—measuring 9.1 on the Richter scale.

Chapter 2

Earthquake in Japan

Minutes after the seismic event, the phone rang in Tom's office. It was the Japanese geological department located in Tokyo. The Japanese official made it clear that they were requesting Tom's assistance to analyze the earthquake event. Tom got off the phone and quickly assembled the people in the office. He spoke to them about the conversation and then started to assemble a team to accompany him to Japan.

In addition to Tom and Rachel, his team consisted of three more people. The first person was Larry Thomas, a thirty-eight-year-old geologist from Colorado who had been on Tom's staff for only three months. Tom thought Larry had an abundance of energy and was very sharp in the area of geology. The second person was Sam Winters, a thirty-two-year-old computer science graduate from California. Tom had hired Sam to help with the monitoring of the computer system at the many locations around the Ring of Fire. Tom thought Sam was low key and did not carry a chip on his shoulder. Tom had talked to people over the years who had degrees in computer science and found that some of them had large egos. The final person on the team was Min-Jun, a twenty-four-year-old Korean with a background in surveying and data mapping. Tom had interviewed several people for the position of surveyor and hired Min because he had graduated with honors and was fluent in English.

Tom and his team took the first plane out of Seoul to Japan to help the government in any capacity they could. They landed in Tokyo and then drove with Japanese government geologists to the areas affected by the tsunami and earthquake. On the drive, Tom could see panic in the people's faces. Many were afraid another earthquake would occur. Given the magnitude of the earthquake, a large part of the island of Japan was affected. Buildings hundreds of miles away had been shaken.

When they arrived at Okuma, Tom was shocked at the devastation the ocean water had caused to the city. He had seen pictures in books of damage caused by earthquakes and tsunamis but seeing the devastation in person set off a whole new set of emotions. His initial shock quickly turned to sadness. Tom saw the people who lived in the city walking around destroyed houses looking for something as small as a family picture. Many of the people were in tears as they held onto their loved ones. Tom set up a small mobile office with Rachel and his team. The office was equipped with desks, file cabinets, tables, and chairs. There was plenty of room in the office to work on their computers and spread paperwork out.

As the government of Japan was trying to evacuate people located around the city, Tom and his team started to measure how far inland the water had pushed from the ocean. He needed to get accurate data, so they used their global positioning satellite gear to pinpoint the coordinates. By mapping the water destruction, they could determine the width and depth of the tsunami in relation to the magnitude. What their data showed them was that the tsunami caused by the earthquake had been roughly thirty feet in height. At that height, cars and buses were easily turned over and washed inland.

Accuracy was important in gathering the data on both on the earthquake and the tsunami, and a lot of driving was needed to survey cities. They traveled hundreds of miles to determine if any distant buildings were showing signs of cracking or shifting. His team put in many hours during the day, basically working sunrise to sunset in the field, then spending several more hours in the evening inputting data and going over the data they had gathered. They ended up spending several weeks in Japan gathering the information.

There were two trailers set up where the team slept and took breaks. The trailers each had two beds and a kitchen area for food preparation. There was also a couch in each trailer, which some team members used for sleeping. Tom's team was not large, so they did not have to sleep in shifts. It turned out that, over the time they were in Japan, nobody was able to get an eight-hour night of sleep; instead, they slept for three to five hours and then got back to work.

Tom and his team entered the conference room. In the room were Japanese officials who had expertise in geology. These meetings had been held every day while Tom and his team were in Japan. Tom started the meeting by discussing the data gathered and the locations they were going to survey. Tom let the Japanese geologists know during the meeting that his team had discovered several buildings in a nearby city that showed signs of cracking.

While the meetings were taking place, Tom's team in Seoul was putting the data obtained by Tom and the others into a computer program. Locations of encroaching water along with descriptions of building damage were some of the many points of data entered into the computer program.

While Tom and Rachel and his team were covering the island of Japan, there were approximately fifteen more members of Tom's staff in Seoul surveying other countries, such as China, the Philippines, Taiwan, Vietnam, Indonesia, and Malaysia, along with South Korea. They were split up in teams of five. In those countries, they specifically traveled to the cities close to the ocean. They checked the monitors to determine if there had been any earthquake or tsunami damage. Due to the number of teams, they could survey only some of the cities.

In each of the seven countries the teams assessed, there were always one or two government representatives of the country who traveled with the teams. They were interested in the way the teams surveyed the cities and obtained the data. The data was shared with these countries, but the final data crunching would occur at the main office in Seoul.

All teams were being coordinated by Tom in Japan. Each five-person team consisted of someone in charge, and that person would speak with Tom daily on their status. Tom wanted to coordinate all teams so they would finish up at about the same time and travel back to Seoul. His team would take a little longer to finish up. He also instructed his teams to locate all power plants in these countries and, additionally, all plants located along the Ring of Fire. The team also needed to determine whether these plants were powered by coal, natural gas, or nuclear energy. These plants were added to a list of critical structures because of the potential effect on the population if they were damaged.

Communication was fortunately not an issue in most countries when the teams were traveling around because there was always someone on the team who could speak one of the languages or could communicate with the country's representatives who were traveling with them. They were not all fluent with languages, and in some places, the team had to communicate using computer translators or old-fashioned translation books. Translating using the books or computers took more time, so a team person would try to minimize this by saying one or two words instead of an entire sentence. This usually worked for them, because rarely more than a sentence or two was needed.

Within the countries surrounding the Ring of Fire, there were tens of millions of people living in cities that were on or close to the ocean. What had taken place off the island of Japan was a picture of what could happen, and this time to a city with more people. If a 9.0 earthquake occurred in the ocean near Shanghai or Taipei, and a thirty-foot or taller wave came in on the shores of these cities, many casualties would occur. And there would be not only casualties, but devastating financial damage to the cities and an undesirable effect on the economy. This was one of the reasons Tom wanted to have his team locate the existing power stations.

If a plant was located near the ocean, a wave of water could take it out of service, causing power outages for many businesses and homes. The loss of life could be in the millions, and the financial impact would be in the tens of billions of dollars.

Chapter 3

Analysis of Data

When Tom arrived back in Seoul from Japan, he called a team meeting with the head of each team to discuss each of the cities and countries in depth. Tom wanted to have a debriefing with the teams so everyone could understand the data and make comments.

Tom started the meeting by discussing the earthquake and tsunami in Japan. He talked about the data gathered during their time in Okuma. The data was extensive, with information on the height of the wave at different locations inland and the damage caused by the earthquake. There was data on the strength of the earthquake inland and the relation between these numbers and the point where the earthquake occurred. The earthquake occurred 110 miles off the coast of northern Japan at a depth of 8,240 feet.

Before starting to talk about the damage in the surrounding areas, Tom asked if anyone had any questions. The head of the team that had gone to Taiwan asked Tom if there had been any warning before the wave rushed inland. Tom said there had been some warning sirens on the shoreline, but not enough to warn the entire population located in the path of the wave. Tom then discussed the damage to the cities and towns located hundreds of miles from the devastation. When the meeting concluded at the end of the day, Tom asked the team to start the process of entering their data into the computer software they used to determine seismic events. He then scheduled another meeting to take place at the end of the week.

The computer software they were using was state of the art. Although it could not predict future events, it could provide percentages of the likelihood of potential events and where they might occur. There were five main areas of input required by the software. The first was the coordinate location of the earthquake. The second was the depth of the earthquake at the coordinates. The third was the time the quake occurred. The fourth was the predominate type of soil within a hundred miles of the earthquake. The fifth was the location on the Ring of Fire related to the five active volcanoes the team monitored.

The better Tom and his team could understand what had happened in the Japan earthquake, the better they would be able to possibly detect any future earthquakes before they occurred. The information the computer generated was a tremendous benefit in pinpointing where a potential earthquake would occur. The satellite specifically in orbit to monitor the area would also help in the pinpointing. Outside influences had been discussed in past meetings and had never been a part of the hard data used by the computers until now.

At the meeting with the team leaders at the end of the week, Tom talked to the others in depth about several "outside sources" that might have played a part in the earthquake and tsunami that occurred in Japan. Tom emphasized that these sources would have to be large to even be considered. Tom talked about deep fracking as the first source.

Fracking is a method used to extract oil that normally cannot be brought up by a traditional oil well. He explained that a solution is injected into the ground that brings up the oil in pockets and cracks. He then asked his team leaders if they were aware of any deep fracking occurring in the areas they had visited that could have caused an earthquake. None of the leaders in the meeting knew of a location around the Ring of Fire. Tom said the relationship between the drilling used in fracking and earthquakes has become more accepted. He talked briefly about the relationship between fracking and earthquakes that were occurring around Oklahoma. "The only other outside source that could contribute to a seismic event would be an underground nuclear detonation," Tom said. "We all know there is only one country performing these tests. Unfortunately, we cannot just arrive in their country and setup monitors," he added.

Mark replied, "Maybe we could sneak across the border and install the monitors without them knowing." Mark was a twenty-eight-year old geology graduate, one of the newest members of the team. The people in the meeting started to laugh. Tom went on to explain that most underground testing would need to be at a depth that would not affect the ground level. Tom knew that the testing of newer, larger nuclear bombs went as deep as 2,400 meters—approximately 7,900 feet or around 1.5 miles—into the ground. Depending on the size of the nuclear bomb, this could shake the underground geological plates. North Korea had been performing testing for the past several years. Because it is a closed country, nobody knew how deep they had been detonating the devices; neither did they know the strength of the bombs. They only knew that these tests were being performed because the same monitors they used to detect earthquakes picked up the activity. Also, the leader of North Korea confirmed the tests after they were run. The monitors Tom and his team checked close to the border between North and South Korea showed readings as high as 3.0, and these readings corresponded to the intentional detonation of devices. Tom thought this testing could have impacted the earthquake and tsunami event in Japan. It was a significant outside source, and he discussed it in depth at the meeting. Tom ended the meeting saying he wanted to analyze the information the computer would produce.

Several weeks later, Tom was handed the results the computer had crunched. The information was in a half-inch-thick bound document. At the beginning of the document were the locations of potential earthquakes in the area around the Ring of Fire. There were five locations to which the computer gave a 50 percent or higher probability of a future earthquake. One of the zones was between the Philippines and southern Japan in the ocean. Of the other four zones, there was a location between Japan and South Korea in the ocean. Two other locations were between Japan and North Korea, and Japan and China, and finally the last location was close to the earthquake that had occurred off the eastern coast of northern Japan.

Tom put the locations on a map of the Ring of Fire so he could see the locations in relation to countries. The size of the earthquakes could not be narrowed down to a single number, but the computer had provided ranges on the Richter scale.

What Tom interpreted from the data was that there could be significant loss of life along the shores if a large tsunami occurred. It was, therefore, extremely important to make sure the early warning systems were in place and functioning correctly. Tom had been working with officials in these countries to have more sirens installed along the shores.

Allowing for the outside influence of the underground testing into the equation, the probability of seismic activity jumped 10 percent. The overall range of the earthquakes did not change, but the increasing probability was significant. Tom wrote the Richter readings on the map corresponding to the locations. He took out a ruler and started lining up the points, hoping to find some type of pattern. With these patterns, Tom could see the locations in relation to the countries. The only way to get concrete data was to set up monitoring systems inside North Korea, which would require approval from the government, and that was not going to happen. The officials Tom had met with in Washington had tried to get approval from a political standpoint, but the ties between the United States and North Korea were nonexistent. Tom had been vocal at these meetings, sometimes raising his voice and pounding his hands on the table. He was convinced it was extremely important to obtain this data from North Korea, and he was not going to back away even in front of his superiors. They even asked China, a country that did have political ties with North Korea, to get them to gain access, but that was not possible. The CIA might have had agents in North Korea, but they were not going to risk their exposure for this mission. Tom thought there was only one way they were going to be able to install monitors, and he would have to do it. He began to think about putting together a team to travel secretly into North Korea and set up secret monitoring stations to gather information on the testing.

Tom was not a spy, but he was intrigued with the thought of going behind enemy lines and gathering the important data he needed. He would have to be trained, along with his small team. The CIA was not going to help in training his team to enter North Korea, and the State Department was not going to officially authorize such a mission. The mission would have been scrubbed entirely if it hadn't been for Tom's determination and insistence that this was so important that it had to be done.

Asia is a hotbed of military mercenaries, and luckily for Tom, one of his team members from South Korea knew of one of them. Tom set up a meeting with the soldier. They would meet at a small café in Seoul on a Friday morning. Tom would wear a red ball cap so the soldier would recognize him. This seemed like minor league spy stuff but was simple enough, and it would work.

Tom arrived at the café and sat down at a table close to the front windows. The café was located at the corner of a main intersection in Seoul, so it was busy. The inside of the café was made to look American with pictures of cities in the US. American music played in the background. A few minutes later, the soldier sat down next to him at the table. "My name is Tom, and I'm with the State Department in Seoul. I was fortunate to have someone in my office who could help me locate you. What is your name? Tell me about your experiences as a soldier."

"My name is Martin," replied the soldier, "and I have lived in South Korea for the past five years. Prior to that I was a navy SEAL. I've spent the last five years working as a mercenary on various missions. "

His military experience with the SEALs was classified, and he would not talk about or, or his missions. He told Tom that, as a mercenary, he had successfully taken a member of the South Korean government into

North Korea, so he knew the best location to enter the country and a route further into the country. Martin told Tom the cost for a mission to North Korea would be $75,000, and the money would have to be all hundred-dollar bills. The amount of money did not faze Tom, and he nodded his head in agreement. The meeting lasted about an hour, and when it was concluded, Martin gave Tom his cell number and told him to contact him if he wanted to put a mission together.

Tom could not wait till Monday to discuss in private with Rachel his meeting with Martin. He called Rachel and met her on Saturday at a public recreation venue called Cheonggyecheon in downtown Seoul to tell her about his meeting. "Rachel, I have been tossing and turning all night waiting to tell you in person about the meeting with the mercenary."

"I can tell you haven't had a good night's rest," she said. "Fill me in on all the details."

Tom began to lay out the details of the meeting, starting with the mercenary's name. He even mentioned the red ball cap he himself had worn and the location in the café where they had talked. "I had a good meeting with Martin. He can help me get into North Korea undetected," he said. He then asked Rachel what she thought.

"The information you could obtain by going on this mission far outweighs the risk," she said.

Tom was relieved when Rachel said that because he knew the two of them were thinking along the same lines. Rachel added that, not only could Tom leave monitors inside North Korea, but he needed to be there when they had another underground detonation. "The first thing would be hard to do, but we would need the help of someone inside the government with knowledge of the testing to complete the second thing," said Tom.

Rachel thought about it for a few seconds then said, "Don't we know someone from North Korea that we met during a seminar?"

"Her name is Kim Yong-Suk," he said. Kim was a geologist from North Korea, and Tom and Rachel had both had conversations with her after one of the conference seminars. "Unfortunately, we can't just pick up the phone and call her at the office because we never know what phones are bugged or who might be listening. Then there's simply the fact that you just can't connect anyway. There's a geologist conference in Tokyo in two weeks. Maybe she'll attend."

On Monday morning at the office, Tom checked the attendees of the conference and saw Kim's name on the list. He had access to the complete list because of his position; he often lectured at these conferences. Tom said, "The main question would be if she would lose her job—or even spend time in prison—if she gets caught helping us a mission."

"I think you summed it all up with that comment," replied Rachel.

Tom needed to contact Kim to find the answer to that question. He needed to make sure they would be in a position during the scheduled conference breaks to have a conversation. Tom was relatively sure she would not be followed during the seminar. She worked in the North Korean government, but she was not in such a high position that her movements would be watched. Tom spent the next two weeks working out what he would say to her when they met. Tom made arrangements to make sure he and Rachel attended the same seminar as Kim so they could approach her during one of the breaks. Tom picked a local bar close to the location of the conference to meet with Kim if she agreed to talk with them.

At the geology conference, at the beginning of a thirty-minute break, Kim Yong-Suk left the room and walked into the hallway. Tom took advantage of the opportunity to talk to her. He and Rachel approached Kim. "Hello," Tom said. "Do you remember me? We talked at a past conference. My name is Tom Vance, and this is Rachel Collins."

"Yes, I do remember both of you," she said.

"Are you enjoying the conference?" asked Tom.

"Yes," she said. "Just being in another country other than North Korea is fun." After an exchange of words, Tom asked Kim if she would meet them for drinks at the bar after the conference was over for the day to discuss an important matter. She was interested in the matter they wanted to discuss and agreed to meet them.

The bar the area was large. There was a single long bar on one side and a stage for concerts on the other side of the room. The bathrooms were in the back, and tables were scattered in the center of the room. Overhead fans were running to disperse the cigarette smoke. Tom, Rachel, and Kim sat at a table, and Tom ordered wine for Rachel and Kim. Tom liked to drink beer. After the waiter delivered their drinks, Tom started the conversation. "Kim, this is what we wanted to talk to you about tonight," Tom said while handing her a map showing monitors along the Ring of Fire. "There are monitors all along the Ring of Fire but no monitors in North Korea," he said. "We also need to obtain data inside North Korea while an underground nuclear test is taking place." Kim was speechless at this point, so Tom laid out the plan to install secret monitors inside North Korea. He did not say how or where this might happen, but he let her know that, without this information, the lives of millions of people could be in jeopardy. He was taking a big risk telling her about their plans, and he knew there were only two answers she could give—yes or no. Specifically, he clarified, "The only thing I'm asking you to do is to let me know when and where the next underground nuclear test will take place."

"I'll find out the information you need and let you know," she said. She added that she would help because she knew that the information could save lives. She was not in the loop regarding the next test, but she knew whom to ask. She could not take a cell phone into the country without suspicion, and phone communications out of the country were sometimes monitored by the government. She would need to somehow obtain this information while she was at the conference in Tokyo. After several drinks, they left the bar. Tom knew that she would contact them again the next day in the hallway of the conference during a break.

The next day, Kim approached Tom during the conference break. Through her contact, she had found that the next test would take place on a Thursday three weeks from then in a remote location approximately thirty-five miles from the town of Kosan. After she said this, Kim slipped Tom a piece of paper on which she had written the exact coordinates of the testing site. Tom thanked her and told her she was saving lives by providing this information.

Chapter 4

The Mission

Tom got on his mobile phone and called Martin, letting him know when the mission had to take place. They would have to be in North Korea during the upcoming underground test. Martin told Tom he would need to spend two days with Tom and his team to train them in the basic skills they'd need for the mission. Tom scheduled the next Saturday and Sunday, mainly because it would not alter his schedule at the State Department, and Rachel was going to stay at the office during the mission; she would be in charge while Tom was gone. Tom requested a one-week vacation so no one would know about his activities or be suspicious. Rachel, of course, knew the reason for this time off. It was unusual to schedule time away on such short notice, but he said that he had a family emergency that needed to be addressed back in America.

There was one more member to add to the team. Tom approached Mark in the office after speaking with Martin on the phone. Mark had been a big addition to the staff in the office. He stood about six feet tall and had brown hair and brown eyes. Tom picked Mark to be on his team for two reasons. First, Mark was the most passionate of the staff members about the importance of monitoring the Ring of Fire. Second, he was an adventure seeker. Mark sat down in the conference room. "Mark, this might sound too much to the point, but I want to find out if you are interested in going on a dangerous mission." This obviously immediately piqued Mark's interest. "I am putting together a team to cross into North Korea and monitor and record data on the next nuclear test." Tom then talked about Martin, the mercenary team member, in detail. After concluding his talk, he asked Mark to provide his thoughts.

"I think this would be a once-in-a-lifetime opportunity to collect data that might help this region," Mark responded. "I'm definitely in on the mission. I was initially a little scared, thinking about getting captured and thrown in prison, but I quickly put that to the side."

Tom reached out, and they shook hands. It was important the team was limited to a total of three people. Tom thought the smaller the team, the easier they could move into the country, and in the worst-case scenario, if they were caught, there would be only a minimal number of people. Tom then told Mark that he would pick him up at seven o'clock on Saturday morning.

On Saturday, Tom arrived in his vehicle at the remote site in the country outside of Seoul with Mark. Tom had brought along a duffle bag containing $75,000 cash, all in hundred-dollar bills. This money was not from the State Department funds because that would be illegal, so he'd had to contact a rich friend to get the funds.

Tom walked around the small remote site. It was an older village, but there were no people living there. The original people had moved to another location years ago. Tom Mark, and Martin would sleep in the abandoned huts during the night. Tom looked to the center of the complex, the main area where the people had a campfire for cooking food. The rocks were arranged neatly in a circle, and a metal bar sat over the fire area.

Martin arrived a short while later in his pickup truck. He jumped out of the driver's seat and handed an empty backpack to Tom and another one to Mark. "What are we going to learn about now?" said Tom.

"Packing the backpack with the essential items is the first task," said Martin. Tom had not camped or hiked much growing up, so he did not know what items they really needed to take with them.

Mark said, "I've camped only once in my life."

Tom felt relieved that another team member had only little camping experience too. The first step took about an hour. Martin had brought everything they would need to take, and soon all the packs were packed for the mission.

Tom thought they should next discuss the path they would take to get close to the test site. He sat down with Martin and Mark at the cooking site and took out a map of North and South Korea. The test site was controlled by the military, but they had to get within only ten miles for the mission. Tom asked Martin, "Where do we need to be to safely cross the border?"

"Crossing the border between North and South Korea will take place close to the South Korean city of Cheorwon," replied Martin. "I used this crossing point the last time I entered North Korea. There are minimal patrols at that point in the border, and it is heavily covered in trees and brush."

Tom marked the location on the map then made a mark where the test site was located, using the coordinates Kim Yong-Suk had given him. He carefully scaled the distance between the two points to determine a total distance. The distance was too far to walk, and Tom looked at Martin and said, "How are we going to get to that area in time?"

Martin put his hands out in a gesture to settle Tom down. "Once we are in North Korea, a farmer who lives in North Korea will pick us up and drive us to the destination point," he said. "I contacted him in South Korea when he drove through the border to South Korea for the North Korea government." Martin had used him on the previous mission and knew he would be in South Korea once a week.

The farmer told Martin that he would help him for the equivalent of two thousand US dollars in North Korean currency. This was a lot of money for the farmer and would help him and his family for many years. Martin had given the farmer a small two-way radio so they could communicate. The radio was small enough that the farmer could hide it when traveling through the border. To cross the border, the team would hide in the back of a pickup truck filled with hay. They would return the same way. "Total time to perform the mission will be four days," said Martin.

"This is a good plan," replied Tom.

One day was for crossing the border and then traveling to the site to install the monitors. They would sleep at the site the first night, and the nuclear test would take place the next day. They did not know what time of day the test would occur, but they were sure it would take place on Thursday according to the information from Kim. After the test, they would again spend the night at the location. They would then travel back to the border on the third day. Tom felt comfortable with the mission Martin had put together, and he did not ask many questions during the briefing.

"What is the next item we should discuss?" Tom said.

"What to wear," Martin answered. "Both of you need to wear brown camouflage so you will blend in with the hay in the back of the farmer's truck. I have the clothing in my truck," said Martin.

"Do we need to wear brown boots?" said Tom.

"Yes, and I have them in my truck as well. I brought several sizes to make sure you will both have shoes that fit. They are combat boots— sturdy and comfortable to wear on long hikes," said Martin.

"Is there anything else we need to wear during the mission?" said Tom.

"You need to carry a knife with a compass and wear a watch. All of our watches will be synchronized so everyone has the same time," Martin said.

"What do we need to talk about next?" Tom said.

"The last item is to go over what to do in case we get caught by North Korean military or police personnel," said Martin. "I think the plan is strong, and the possibility of getting caught is small, but it does need to be discussed. If you are interrogated," Martin said, "tell them the truth."

"Tell them the truth?" said Tom.

"The truth will ensure that all of our stories are the same and there is nothing wrong with our mission except that we are illegally in North

Korea," replied Martin. Tom nodded his head in agreement. "Let them know that we are in their country to monitor the underground testing and to set up remote monitors. If they instruct us to show them where the monitors are located, agree to do that. There is no reason to not answer their questions, but do not tell them about the data on the flash drive," said Martin.

"I'm in charge of the flash drive," said Tom. "I'll hide it somewhere on the ground if we are captured."

It was getting late in the evening, so Tom, Mark, and Martin prepared a flame-grilled steak dinner in the village over an open fire. "Martin, who is your favorite college football team?" Tom asked.

"Ohio State, definitely. How about you, Tom?"

"Stanford, because I'm an alumnus."

"They are both great teams, but UCLA is the best college football team," said Mark.

Tom laughed and said, "You're saying that because you graduated from there."

Tom and Mark called it a night at around ten, as they planned on getting up at around seven so they would have time for one more briefing with Martin before they drove back to Seoul.

On Sunday morning, Tom and Mark woke. Together they prepared coffee and scrambled eggs over the campfire. Martin was already awake and had the campfire going for the food and coffee. As they sat around the campfire, Martin went over one last time the location and the time they were to meet him. They only needed to be dressed and have their accessories, while Martin would have the backpacks. Tom would bring the two miniature earthquake monitors and the laptop, so Martin could put these items in a separate backpack. Tom and Mark left the village at around eleven to drive back to Seoul.

On the day of the mission, Tom called Rachel to make sure she did not need anything more before he left. "Rachel," he said, "we are starting the mission, heading close to the border.

"You know I'll be worried about you," she replied.

"I know, but the plan we've put in place is precise, and I don't have any concerns. I'll call you as soon as I get back across the border. Take care of the staff while I'm gone."

"I will," she said. "And please call me when you are safe."

Tom and Mark left Seoul at around one in the afternoon to drive north to the meeting point with Martin. The highway out of Seoul was busier than usual at this time so they had to sit through several traffic jams. During these periods when they were driving slowly, Tom thought about the mission. He had a small amount of anxiety about crossing into North Korea, but the overall result of getting data far outweighed this feeling.

They arrived at the location when the sun was setting. Tom and the team spent roughly thirty minutes at the location before heading out on the mission. It would take twelve miles of hiking to make it across the border and another five miles inward to the meeting point with the farmer. This would make the walk around six to seven hours, probably a little longer because of the terrain and the necessary breaks they would take. If they left at seven, they should be at the meeting point with the farmer between one and two o'clock in the morning. They were to meet the farmer at six in the morning, so they had a float of approximately four hours in case it took longer to walk the distance.

The terrain was what Tom expected. It was flat for roughly two-thirds of the trip, and then hilly for the remainder. Tom was getting winded by the time the team made it to the meeting point at close to three in the morning, so they found an area covered by grass and brush and sat down to rest. Martin said they could close their eyes for several hours and get some rest. After the long hike, it was easy for Tom to doze off, and Mark did the same. Martin, being in the military, closed his eyes but was a light sleeper. He knew he would wake up if he heard anything in the area.

The North Korean farmer arrived on time with his hay truck. Martin slipped him the money that he had requested, and they all got in the back of the truck under the hay, hidden from view. The drive to the location took several hours as the farmer took less-traveled roads to avoid any police and military patrols. The roads were not smooth, and the team members bounced around constantly during the trip.

When they reached the location, the team members got out of the truck, and Tom waved the farmer off. Tom thought about his promise to be back in two days, and he hoped he would.

At the site, Tom and Mark started to set up the monitoring equipment. Tom pointed at a location and said, "The first monitor will be located there." There were two stations, which they set up within a hundred yards of each other. Tom verified that the equipment was able to detect activity. Tom looked over at Martin to check on him. "Any activity, Martin?"

Martin was constantly surveying the terrain with his binoculars, keeping an eye out for any North Korean activity. "All clear," he replied.

When the two stations were up and running, Tom punched in the coordinates on his computer, but he needed to activate the signal from Seoul, just in case they were detected somehow by the North Koreans. Everything was running correctly. The mini stations were run by small, rechargeable, solar-powered batteries, so they could run continuously. During the test the next day, they would use the stations on site, transferring the data directly to Tom's computer and backing up on the flash drive. The flash drive data would be their only priority if they were caught.

When it got dark, the team members set up their perimeter closely, all three of them within ten feet of each other. "Now would be a great time to eat dinner," said Tom.

"I have delicious MREs for us to eat tonight," replied Martin. They could not start a fire for fear it would be noticed, but the "meals ready to eat" could be heated with special flameless heaters.

"Each person will take a four-hour shift watching for lights or people," said Tom. "Martin, you take the last watch so you can get some sleep right away. I'll take first watch, and, Mark, you take the second."

In the middle of the morning, while Mark was on shift, he saw a vehicle's lights in the distance getting closer to the campsite. When the vehicle was within one mile of their location, Mark woke the others. They all watched for several minutes until the vehicle turned onto another road and drove away.

Chapter 5

Nuclear Testing in North Korea

K im arrived at the test site and entered the main command center, the location of the bomb, including equipment that was tied to it. Her senior scientist position in geology with the North Korean government put her on the short list. She looked at the aerial pictures showing the test site. She studied engineering drawings of the tunnel and the device. Above her head, a series of television monitors were set up, each focused on a different area of the detonation site. She knew her duty during the test was to record the magnitude the earth shook during the nuclear detonation underground. Additional information she would need included the depth of the detonation and the size of the nuclear bomb. This was all she was supposed to record and do in her capacity during the test.

There were around thirty-five people in the building and the area around the building. Some of the people were in charge of the testing, but most of the people were military officers only there for the test. A general briefed Kim on the activities for the day. He told her there would be two detonations during the day. The first would occur at eleven o'clock in the morning and the second at three o'clock in the afternoon. He then instructed her to work with one of the personnel in the building during the tests.

Kim had brought with her a testing machine that probably was fifty years old, and it was bulky and hard to carry. This machine would spit out a piece of paper imprinted with data it recorded; it looked similar to a lie detector machine. After analyzing the data, the experts could determine the size of the shock to within 0.2 on the Richter scale. They had drilled a shaft to a depth of a mile and a half and had inserted a bomb that was thirty-five megatons in size.

Kim looked around at the people in the building. Everyone talked amongst themselves, waiting for the leader of the country to arrive. Kim looked at the clock. It was ten thirty in the morning when the leader arrived at the site along with additional government personnel. Kim knew the test was not going to start until the leader arrived; he was always present for the tests. Kim stood in line with everyone in the building waiting to shake the leader's hand. She was nervous because she had never been in a room with the leader of the country. She shook his hand, and he asked, "What is your name? And why are you here today?"

"My name is Kim Yong-Suk, and I'm here today to monitor the ground movement after the detonation," she said. He smiled and moved to the next person.

At ten forty-five, a clock in the building was activated and started to count down to zero. Sirens were sounded to warn everyone that the detonation was going to occur within minutes, and people started to run inside buildings onsite. The actual location of the shaft was approximately two miles from the main control building, and Kim could actually see the structure above the shaft. She looked above at the three monitors showing the structure above the device.

The clock was running down to zero, and when it hit ten seconds, some of the officers started to count down out loud. At zero, the ground shook for a few seconds, and the hanging lights in the main building started to move back and forth. The floorboards started to move, and the people in the building had to hold onto each other or something in the building to steady themselves. Kim was watching the machine as the needle moved up and down. She could tell without a ruler that the detonation caused a high Richter scale reading.

Kim cheered along with the group when everything went as planned. She saw people shaking hands with each other and talking about the detonation. She retrieved the data from her machine and sat down at a table for further analysis. She determined the detonation had caused a 4.3 earthquake at the distance they were from the bomb.

Kim knew there was another test to be performed in the afternoon, and she watched the people in the building walk over to another structure around noon. "What's inside the building?" she asked a technician in the room.

"There is an entire spread of food," he said. About an hour later, Kim looked up and saw the site personnel going back to work at their individual jobs. She watched the military leaders, along with the leader of the country, walk over and board a bus. Kim was curious where they were traveling in the bus, but she needed to concentrate on the data she had obtained. She wondered if Tom had recorded the same Richter scale reading.

It was around two fifteen in the afternoon when Kim saw the bus of officers and the leader arrive back at the main building for the second test. As with the first test, the depth and size of the charge were the same. At three o'clock the second detonation occurred, and again it shook the main building. Kim determined the readings were almost identical to the first test, with an earthquake of 4.3 on the scale. She stayed at the building for another forty-five minutes, entering the test data into her computer. She then got into a car and left the site. She traveled back to Pyongyang, the capital of North Korea.

Tom got up and checked the two monitors to make sure they were still functioning correctly. *Both online and functioning correctly,* he thought. Aloud he said, "If everything goes on as planned for today, we should receive some good data, don't you agree, Mark?"

Mark nodded his head in agreement.

"These monitors are approximately twelve and a half miles from the test site based on my calculations," said Tom. For most of the morning, Tom kept his eyes glued to his computer, anxiously waiting for any movement. At a little after eleven in the morning, the ground shook enough for Tom to easily feel the movement. "Wow!" said Tom "Did you feel that, Mark?"

"Yes. What do you think that was on the Richter scale?"

"I think it was about a three," replied Tom. The data began to pour in on Tom's laptop computer. The movement of the earth had lasted for only a few seconds, but that was more than enough to get the data. Being as close as they were, the computer told Tom that it was a 4.2 on the Richter scale.

Tom was shocked that the reading was that high and kept looking at the number to reassure that he was correct. He walked to both monitors and checked the readings, and they were the same as the reading on his computer. In his mind, he was running over the number and how it might change the overall predictions from the main computer software. "I was thinking this information might increase the probability of future earthquakes occurring by five percent and the magnitude by point two on the Richter scale," he said.

"I agree with your assumption," said Mark. "And without this information, we would have never known." He typed his thoughts and experience into a file on his computer after the earthquake occurred so he could go over it again back in Seoul.

Tom did some final calibration on the monitors before sunset. Dinner again consisted of MREs, and Tom and the team sat around for an hour talking to each other about what had taken place during the day and what this might mean to the Ring of Fire and the other countries.

This evening, there were a few more cars in the distance but nothing heading in their direction. Both evenings there were clear skies and a bright moon, but it was a little cold. Their camouflage clothing provided a decent amount of protection against colder temperatures. In the middle of the night the temperatures got down to sixty-two degrees, so sleeping was not difficult. Each of them had a warm cap to wear to keep their heads warm, and they had insulated gloves. Tom thought to himself that at least it was not raining; being wet would be unpleasant. The farmer would be picking them up at seven in the morning to take them back close to the border.

The team woke at around six and packed their backpacks for the trip to the border. The farmer arrived at seven as planned, and they again hid under the hay in the back of the pickup truck. Tom was in the back, so he could not tell if the farmer was taking the same route he'd taken before. About twenty minutes into the trip, Tom heard the sound of a tire blowing out. The vehicle stopped, and Tom got out of the back to see what tire was damaged. He looked around. The terrain was flat, so he would be able to see someone coming from a mile away. Tom asked the farmer in English where the spare tire was. The farmer seemed to know what he was asking even though he did not speak a word of English. The farmer pointed to the underside of the pickup bed. Martin and Mark got out of the truck. "I got this," Tom said to Martin.

"Are you sure you don't need some help with the tire change?" said Martin.

"This will be a piece of cake," Tom said. He rolled the tire up to the front of the truck and jacked the front left side of the truck up. Martin, along with Mark, stood and watched as Tom removed the tire and installed the spare. It took less than fifteen minutes, and the truck was ready to go again. As they hopped into the back of the truck again, Martin couldn't help himself and said to Tom, "Not bad for a geologist." Mark started laughing.

"You don't have to be a navy SEAL to change a tire," said Tom. The three of them hid under the hay for the remainder of the trip.

When the truck stopped and Tom heard the farmer bang on the back of the truck bed, he knew they had arrived at the pickup point. Tom shook the farmer's hand and thanked him in English. The farmer drove away, and Tom and his team walked to the same location where they had stayed during the start of the mission. The trip across the border would be done at night, so they had several hours to wait hidden in the grassy area. "Why don't we set up the same shifts as before to keep lookout until it is dark?" said Tom.

"Sounds good," replied Martin.

Later in the afternoon, Tom heard the sound of a vehicle driving in their direction. He could tell that it was a large vehicle by the loud sound it made as it approached. "Everyone get deeper in the grass," Tom yelled. The three men ran about thirty feet deeper into the grass. When the vehicle approached the closest point between Tom and his team, they all lay very still. Tom watched as the military truck passed by only a hundred yards from their location. The vehicle drove past them on the road, the occupants never noticing the team. After it had passed, Tom was the first to stand up. "Wow!" he said. "That got my heart pumping pretty fast. How about you, Martin?"

"All of those years in the military, and I still get a rush."

"Let's just remain in this location until dark," said Tom.

When it was starting to get dark, the team took off toward the border, taking the same path they had used at the beginning of the mission. Around one hour into the hike back to South Korea, the men entered an area where there were many trees. It was difficult at this point in the hike to work their way through. Each member of the team had a small flashlight, which was strong enough to show about five feet of the path in front of him, but not so strong that it could be spotted from a distance.

The only thing they had to be aware of was the fact that they could not see well through the trees; in fact, soldiers could be twenty-five feet from them and they would not know.

Tom walked into an area with many trees and was spotted by North Korean soldiers. The soldiers had cleared an area in the trees and stationed a vehicle equipped with a strong spotlight. "Halt and put your hands up," said one of the soldiers.

Their machine guns were pointed at the team, but the soldiers did not have a clear view. The spotlight on the vehicle lit up the area, but the many trees made tracking the team difficult.

"Run! Run!" Tom yelled. The soldier in the back of the vehicle moved the light so it shone where Tom, Martin, and Mark were running. The North Koreans fired shots in their direction, but the bullets were hitting trees. The soldiers ran after the team. For about hundred yards, the three team members remained far enough ahead to feel safe, but then they ran into an area where they had to backtrack. The area in front and to the left and right of them was a small hill. It was difficult enough to climb without pressure, but in this case, they did not have the time.

Tom saw the soldiers coming closer, and he made the decision to throw the flash drive device into the wooded area. The steel case containing the flash drive was water resistant. The soldiers did not notice him throwing the container, mainly because they were running and the lights on their guns were bouncing up and down. By this time, the soldiers were ten feet from the team members and would clearly be able to shoot them if they ran again.

Tom, Martin, and Mark put their hands up, and one of the soldiers pulled their hands behind their backs and secured them with handcuffs. The soldiers pointed their guns at their captives and marched them back to the area where the vehicle was located. One of the soldiers got on the radio to tell his superior that they'd caught three people and to send another vehicle to transport them back to headquarters. It was about an hour before another vehicle arrived. This vehicle was a truck, but in the bed area was a cage constructed from a series of posts.

While his team were being put into the back of the truck, Tom was looking back at the area where he'd thrown the canister with the data. The North Koreans were walking around the capture area with flashlights, looking to see if the captives might have dropped something. The area where Tom threw the canister was approximately twenty feet from where they were looking, which relieved Tom. In addition to this, the canister had rolled another five feet down a slope and was mainly covered by leaves. The North Koreans never went into the area where the canister was located.

Tom was put in the back of the vehicle, and they spent an hour—at least in Tom's mind—driving until the vehicle completely stopped. The vehicle had to stop at the main gate so the soldiers there could verify the soldiers driving the vehicle. Once they were granted permission to pass the gate, the vehicle took the team to a building in the center of the compound. There were many soldiers walking around the area, along with tanks and military equipment. Tom and the team were led up a long set of stairs into the building and placed in a locked room with their hands cuffed to a table.

Chapter 6

Captured and Interrogated by North Korea

B y the time Tom was brought into the military building and hand-cuffed to the table it was one o'clock in the morning. Tom waited for someone to enter the room, but an additional hour passed before anyone came. The door finally opened, and a military officer walked into the room. A few seconds later, two more soldiers walked into the room. Tom was still handcuffed to the table when the officer sat down on the other side.

Tom thought that the officer was probably from the main military complex located Pyongyang. The officer spoke to Tom in English, asking him first what his name was. Tom told the officer his name and then waited for the next question to be asked. The officer then asked him if he was in the military, to which Tom replied he was a geologist and not in the military. The officer asked why he was in North Korea. Tom said he was there to get seismic data during an underground nuclear test. The officer asked specifically if there anything he needed to be aware of with regard to the data. Tom said the tests had shaken the ground to such an extent that the activity recorded a 4.2 on the Richter scale. He told the officer that he had written papers related to the Ring of Fire and the effects of earthquakes and tsunamis. After listening to Tom's answer, the officer asked if they had been close to the test site, and where exactly they were located to gather this information. Tom replied they were about twelve miles away from the test site in the hills.

About thirty minutes had passed during the question-and-answer session, and Tom was thirsty. He asked the officer if he could have a cup of water. Because Tom had been cooperating with his questions, the officer opened the door and shouted down the hall for a cup of water. He waited with the door open until another soldier brought him the water. Closing the door to the interrogation room, he put the cup on the table within Tom's reach. There was some slack in the handcuffs attached to the table, so he was able to pick up the cup and take a drink.

The officer then asked if they had taken any pictures at their location. Tom replied that they were only there to record the data, and nobody took pictures of the area. The officer then asked if they had left anything behind at the site. Tom's answer to that was yes, there were two small earthquake monitors located at the site, which they could activate when they got back at Seoul.

Taking it a step further, the officer asked Tom whether he had the coordinates of the location of the monitors. Tom told the officer to reach into his inside pocket where they would find a piece of paper on which he had written the coordinate numbers. Tom could tell by the officer's facial expressions that he was a little upset . The reason he was upset was that the soldiers who had caught Tom and his friends should have done a better job checking his clothing and should have discovered this piece of paper.

The question then turned to whether the team had hidden any data before being captured. Tom had been up front and honest with all the questions until this question was asked. He replied to the officer that the only items they had were in their clothes and in their backpacks, and this included the laptop.

As far as the officer knew, they had hiked across the border to the site to gather their information and then hiked back. It was a long distance, but it certainly could be done. Tom was not going to say anything about the farmer and the help he had provided to the team. The team members were never asked if they'd had any additional help, specifically anyone from North Korea.

The officer asked Tom if his superiors in South Korea were aware of this mission, to which he replied that they were not aware. The mission was off the books, and nobody other than himself and his two friends were in the loop. He did say that a group of former soldiers helped with setting up the mission, only because he could sense the officer was starting to think he was not cooperating.

At this point in the interrogation, the officer was somewhat confident that Tom was telling him the truth and there was no secret mission to take pictures of military sites or to steal North Korean secrets.

The officer then instructed a soldier to take Tom to a holding cell located inside the building. The soldier walked with Tom down a series of hallways and stairs until they arrived at the cells. Tom counted six cells, so he thought that Martin and Mark would ultimately end up there also. In Korean, the soldier told an officer to open the cell and then close it after Tom was inside. The cell was not entirely empty; there was a cot with a pillow and sheets for sleeping. There was no sink, only a toilet, and there was only one cot, so Tom thought he would be in this cell alone. The cells were next to each other, so he might be able to talk to Martin and Mark.

Martin and Mark were brought individually to the interrogation room where the officer had questioned Tom. The officer repeated the same questioning to determine if the answers were the same.

After the officer was finished with the interrogations, he concluded that the answers from all three of the captives were honest, and the mission had only been carried out for the earthquake data.

Both Martin and Mark were put into the cell next to Tom. None of the men had any concept of time or how long the interrogations had taken, but they all felt that it must be almost morning.

Tom asked Mark and Martin what questions they had been asked and what they had said, trying to find out if their stories were the same. He was relieved they'd given the same answers, and they were fortunate they had discussed how they would behave in this situation before the mission. Tom tried to rest for a short period of time, but soon he was awakened by the sound of opening cell doors.

Through the light in the window Tom could see from his cell, he knew it was morning. The guard brought a plate of potatoes with a piece of bread and a tin cup filled with water. After they were finished, the doors to all three cells were opened, and the soldiers escorted the prisoners out of the building and into the back of the same vehicle that had brought them to the complex. Before they left the complex, a soldier gave each of them a bottle of water for the trip. Tom rode in the back of the vehicle for several hours until the area started to look familiar. Using the coordinates from the piece of paper, the driver was able to take them to the exact location the team had been located. When the truck came to a stop, Tom got out of the back of the vehicle. In English, the officer instructed him to locate the earthquake monitors. Tom started walking to the first monitor with the soldiers while Martin and Mark stood by the truck. He walked up to the first monitor, and the soldiers quickly picked it up and took it back to another vehicle. Tom then walked to the second monitor, which the soldiers also removed. He pointed out to the officer where they'd slept during the night. The matted grass proved his story.

Tom got back in the vehicle, and they drove off with several military vehicles in front and several more behind them. The vehicles started to head in a different direction. When the vehicles arrived at a gate, the soldiers honked the horn. Tom could see that it was a large city with the buildings and cars driving down the roads.

Entering the compound, Tom could see many buildings, and when they stopped, he got out of the vehicle and stood in front of a building. A North Korean flag blew in the breeze from a flagpole out in front by the steps. The soldiers escorted him into building. He was put into a holding cell again, where he remained for a while. Eventually, Tom was taken from the holding cell into another room where a different officer questioned him this time. The questions were mainly the same ones he'd been asked before. The North Korean officer wanted to make sure the answers were the same as his previous ones.

Kim Yong-Suk was at her desk in Pyongyang when she got a call from an officer in the military. "Hello," she said.

"This is General Do-Won," he said.

"Yes, General. How can I help you?"

"We have captured three men in this country trying to monitor the ground activity while we performed our last underground nuclear test. During the interrogations, it was determined that one of the individuals by the name of Tom Vance had written papers on the Ring of Fire." Kim started to get nervous. "Do you know this person through your travels outside the country to earthquake seminars?"

"Yes, I know who he is because he gave a talk on the Ring of Fire," she said. By now, Kim started to sweat thinking the next question was going to expose her and the help she had given to Tom.

"I need you to come to the military complex in the next hour so you can verify who he is," the general said.

"I'll be there in an hour." Kim hung up the phone and took a deep breath. She did not know for sure if she had been exposed through the interrogations, but she thought the general's questions would have alerted her if she had been.

Kim finished some work and left her office and drove to the military complex where the three captives were located. Her mind was racing between helping the captives and what they might do to her if they found out she had helped. She also started to get a little paranoid, thinking that the government might already know she'd helped them. How was she to know what had been discussed during the interrogations? The drive took about twenty minutes. When she arrived at the front gate, she was directed to the building with the flagpoles out front.

Inside the building, she was escorted to a room where a one-way glass took up part of one wall. They could see in, but the person in the other room could not see out. Inside the room was Tom, sitting in a chair. The officer asked Kim if she had ever seen him in her travels outside the country. She replied that she had seen him when she attended a seminar where he was speaking about the Ring of Fire. She said the seminar took place recently in Tokyo. She was nervous, but the officer did not seem to notice. She kept thinking that at any time they would arrest her and haul her off to jail and interrogation.

Kim was given Tom's laptop computer, which only had the recorded data on it and no other information, such as the scope of the mission. Tom had been more than willing to provide the password during the interrogation, knowing it was the only data on the computer. The officer instructed Kim to look at the data on the computer and confirm that seismic monitoring was the only thing they had been doing. She took the laptop and sat down at a table in the room. She then opened the program up for review. There was more data on the laptop than what she had to work with at the test site. She noted a 4.2 reading on the Richter scale, which was close to her number. After spending about fifteen minutes looking at the information, she told the officer it was earthquake data on the computer and nothing more. She was thanked for her work and instructed to leave and go back to her job.

She was relieved when the officer told her to leave the building. It was at that point that she knew the three captives had never said anything about her involvement. When she got back to her office, there was roughly an hour left in the workday, so she took this time going over the data from the nuclear tests. She knew it was 4.2 at their location and it was 4.3 at the test site. She also saw on the computer the distance they had been away from the detonation.

When it was time to leave the office, she was in a hurry to leave, and when she got home, she sat in her favorite chair thinking about the day and wondering what would happen to Tom. Would they spend the rest of their lives in prison or would the government eventually release them back to South Korea? She was hoping they would release them, knowing they were only in the country to gather data to help in future predictions of earthquakes. She had heard over the years what prison was like in North Korea. The life expectancy of anyone in prison was shortened by many years.

Chapter 7

Negotiations for Release

Inside their prison cell, Tom started to talk about the possibility of getting released someday. He wondered if they were going to spend the rest of their lives in a prison. "I think we have a good chance of getting released and making it back to South Korea," he said.

"I don't know," said Martin. "The North Koreans take any matter like this seriously, especially since we snuck across their border."

"I have to agree with Tom," said Mark.

"What we did was not that serious," added Tom. "I think that, because we told them the truth, they will release us, but first they might try to get some concessions from South Korea or the US. I'm a firm believer that honesty is the best policy. The only criminal part of our mission was entering the country without permission," he said.

At the time they didn't know if officials in South Korea knew they had been captured, and, if they did know, if they were working on their release.

Rachel was in her office when she got a phone call from John Williams with the Department of State. He started the conversation by saying that

Tom had been captured in North Korea, and that negotiations had begun for their release. Rachel asked John if the team members were in good health, but John could not answer that question. He said that they had only received news of their capture through an email. They had replied to North Korea that they would like to have a picture of the captives to confirm their identity. "Did you know Tom was in North Korea?" John asked.

"Yes, I knew they were in North Korea. The only reason they went on this mission was to gather information from the underground nuclear test. It was so important to obtain the data. It could potentially help millions of people," she said.

"I understand the reason for the data, but Tom should have worked with us to obtain it," said John.

"He did try to reason with Washington officials to go through proper channels but was shut down by them," she said. "He felt this was his only choice."

"I have to make another call to Washington, so stay in Seoul because you will be contacted again," said John.

Rachel hung up the phone and immediately started to think about Tom and what sort of condition he might be in.

Later in the afternoon, Rachel received a phone call from John. "There is a team of diplomats en route from Washington. I need you to be ready tonight to accompany me to meet them. I'll pick you up at your office at seven o'clock so we can drive to the airport."

"I'll be ready," replied Rachel.

When the plane landed in Seoul, Rachel was there to meet Steven, who was a diplomat with the US State Department, and ride with him and his staff members to the State Department. At the State Department, the delegation and John sat down to discuss in detail the information they had obtained and what they could do to get the team released. John informed them the reason they had been in North Korea and the importance of the information. Steven understood but was not happy that Tom and his team had decided to go rogue and, on top of that, get caught. He thought they could have taken more diplomatic avenues to get the data. Rachel quickly jumped to Tom's defense and said he had tried other avenues.

The office of the Department of State in Seoul was busy addressing the capture and what possible actions they could take to get them released. Every idea would be discussed no matter how crazy it might sound. Rachel sat in on a meeting with John to discuss with his staff possible schemes they could dream up do to get them released.

John received an email through diplomatic channels. Attached were several pictures of Tom, Mark, and Martin. He made a print of one of the pictures of Tom and handed it to Rachel when he arrived in the conference room. Rachel looked at the picture of Tom and smiled, relieved that he was alive and looked in good health. John handed the pictures of the three men to Steven and his group. "Looks like they are in good health. Would you agree, Rachel?" said Steven.

"His face looks good, and he looks happy," she said.

Steven switched gears and said, "We need to discuss what their demands are for their release. Several North Koreans have been caught and imprisoned in South Korea for spying. A prisoner exchange could take place."

At the prison in Pyongyang, Tom took things on a day-to-day basis. He was being interrogated daily, but he was being treated well. The door opened, and two soldiers walked into the room. They opened up Tom's cell and took him to a room. Inside the room he was instructed to sit down. An officer came in and took his picture. This was the first time Tom thought there could be some type of negotiations going on between North Korea and South Korea. He thought this was the reason for taking their pictures—to show that they were alive and well. After a series of pictures, he was taken back to his cell.

The next morning, Rachel arrived at the State Department and sat down in the conference room. John entered the room and proceeded to inform Steven he had just got off the phone with a South Korean official. In his hand was an email that contained the demands from the North. Rachel listened as John started to read the email. In exchange for the release of the three team members, three individuals currently locked up in a South Korean prison would be released. Steven then turned to the Koreans in the room and asked them to contact the person in the government who could grant a release.

Later in the afternoon, Rachel watched as the two diplomats from the South Korean government entered the conference room and sat down to discuss the release of the prisoners. She had spent hours thinking about the exchange, wondering if it would actually take place. One of the diplomats said that it would not be a problem to release two of the men, but one of the prisoners had shot and killed a South Korean officer during his capture. Rachel's stomach started to sink with worry. Would they release the prisoner involved in this crime? The South Korean diplomats thought an answer would come in a day. The diplomats left the office and said they would return when an answer was determined. John and Steven discussed the potential price this exchange would have on the relationship between South Korea and America as Rachel listened. They concluded that it would be strained some but not by much.

The next day, at around eleven in the morning, the representatives from South Korea arrived at the office with the answer Rachel had been hoping for. The answer was yes, they would release the prisoner, and he would be a part of the exchange.

The State Department crafted an email and sent it to North Korea, agreeing with the demands. It would take another day to determine when and where the exchange was going to happen.

Eventually it was determined that the exchange would take place the following Monday at eight o'clock in the morning at Panmunjom along the Armistice Line. The location was a very familiar location where soldiers from North Korea and South Korea were close to each other, separated only by the border. Rachel had feelings of joy after hearing where the exchange would take place.

There were two additional points that John needed to set before the exchange. Rachel listened as he put a call in to the general in charge of the US troops in South Korea. He explained that the exchange was going to occur at the Armistice Line and needed him to notify all military personnel that would be involved. The other phone call was to arrange for the prisoners in South Korea to be released and transported to Panmunjom by Sunday night.

On Sunday afternoon at the prison in Pyongyang, the North Korean soldiers entered the prison area and escorted Tom and his two friends out of the building into a truck. This truck did not have bars in the back; instead, it was totally enclosed. Tom did not have any idea what was happening. In his mind, he was thinking everything from getting released to heading to an official prison.

None of the soldiers would say anything, so the three of them discussed their thoughts in the back of the vehicle. "Where do you think were heading?" said Tom.

"I think that we're going to border," replied Martin.

"I think we are going to the border also," said Tom. "What do you think, Mark?"

"I would have thought prison, but after they took our pictures, I thought some type of negotiation was taking place."

When they arrived at the destination, it was dark, so they could not get a fix on their location. They were escorted to a building, and all three were put into a locked room. There was a table in the room and chairs, but all three of them sat on the floor with their backs against the wall.

On Monday morning at six o'clock, Tom and the others were given a small protein bar and some water. It wasn't a lot, but it was enough to start the day. They were led into a room with a toilet and sink and were given razors and foam so they could shave. When they had finished, Tom was feeling good, thinking that they could be going back to South Korea.

At seven thirty, Tom, Mark, and Martin were escorted outside the building. Now that it was daylight, Tom could see the buildings in the area, but he still could not determine their location. They walked for about ten minutes until they could see the Armistice Line. Arriving at the checkpoint, they stood next to the soldiers until they could see three individuals on the South Korean side. Tom, Martin, and Mark started to walk with the soldiers toward the South Korean side. The soldiers from the South started to walk toward them. When they got to the middle at the border, the exchange occurred. Tom walked with the South Korean soldiers into a building, where he was met by Steven and John, along with US military officers.

Tom was led into a room for debriefing. He was asked where he had been held and how they had been treated. The debriefing lasted several days, during which time he could roam freely in the building, but he could not leave. The main thing Tom had on his mind was how he could retrieve the flash drive that he'd pitched before capture. By now, he thought the North Korean military would have increased the presence in that area.

During the debriefing, Tom had detailed his actions when they were captured and mentioned that the canister with the drive was lying on the ground in the area. He was very outspoken regarding retrieving the drive and how important to the whole region it was to get that information.

After several days, Tom was released and headed to Seoul. He could not stop thinking that he, and possibly Mark, would end up losing their jobs because of their actions. Sleeping in his own bed helped him relieve some of the worrisome thoughts in his head. At home, he sat on the couch in his living room and called Rachel to let her know he was back in Seoul. "I'm so relieved you a back home again," she said.

"It has been an emotional experience," he replied.

"I was able to sit in on all the meetings taking place for your release," she said.

"I bet that was a roller coaster ride."

"Yes, it was, and I can't wait to see you tomorrow. Are you coming to the office in the morning?" asked Rachel

"I'll be there first thing in the morning."

"Have a good night's sleep," she said.

"I'll definitely sleep well. Good night."

The next day, Tom headed to the office and talked to Rachel further about his mission and the data they were able to get from the testing. He had thought the canister and flash drive would be lost because nobody was going to retrieve it, especially after what had taken place. The main concern on Tom's mind was whether he was going to lose his job with the State Department. He had a conversation with Kyle Wright in Washington, and it was up in the air whether he would keep his job. Another two weeks passed before there was official communication from Washington. Tom's position was too important. He would remain in Seoul as head of the department. Another week passed before he received a call from John Williams.

Chapter 8

The Quest to Recover Hidden Data

John Williams called Tom, first to check on how he was doing, but mainly to discuss the canister he'd hidden before being captured. Tom had told him in detail the location of his capture and how close the data was to that location, just off to the side in the trees. Tom had explained all of this while he was being debriefed, but John wanted to talk to him one on one. "This information is too important to leave it on the ground in North Korea," explained Tom. "John, you need to get on the phone with Washington and somehow get approval to retrieve it."

"Way ahead of you on this one," John said. "Washington has given the green light, and a team is being assembled. I need you to be on this team and help them locate the canister. Are you in or out?" said John.

"I'm definitely in on the mission," replied Tom.

"Arrive at the State Department at eight in the morning for a briefing." John ended the call.

Tom arrived at the State Department in Seoul and was escorted to a room where a meeting was to begin about the mission. The general in charge of the troops in South Korea took the lead during the meeting. Also involved in the meeting were officials with South Korea, both in the military and with the government.

Tom looked at the satellite pictures of the area where they were captured, but they showed only several hundred yards in each direction. It was critical they locate the canister to within feet; otherwise, they would spend too much time looking for it, and that would increase the chance of being caught. Tom picked up a pencil and marked on the picture a location that would narrow it down to approximately twenty feet. "This is great!" the general said. "I have put together an elite team of Green Berets to accompany you on the mission."

"Just give me the location and time to show up, and I'll be there," replied Tom.

Tom learned during the meeting about the equipment they would be using on the mission. They would have up-to-date satellite images showing locations of the North Korea military and would have locators showing their positions. Also, they would have state-of-the-art communication systems so they could talk to each other and to the main command in South Korea.

Tom was instructed to arrive at a military base not far from the border the following Monday. He was not to bring anything with them; he was only to show up at seven in the morning at the base. Tom was not allowed to talk to Rachel about this mission. It was classified secret, and nobody was to talk to anyone about any part of the mission. The military and government could not risk someone from North Korea finding out about what they were going to do, which would cause them to increase the military on their side of the border.

The Sunday before the mission, Tom was nervous for some reason. In his mind, he knew that this mission was planned and monitored in much more detail than the previous mission, but this did not alleviate his thoughts about the time they were captured and the time they spent in prison. He had to redirect those thoughts to the current mission and how important the canister with the drive was to the stability of the region. He fell asleep with these thoughts going through his head.

On Monday morning, Tom approached the main gate at the military compound and gave the soldier his identification. The soldier told him to head toward the tallest building in the compound. Tom drove off and, a few minutes later, arrived at the building. The soldier at the gate had called ahead to let them know he was coming, and there was a soldier in front of the building to meet him. Tom got out of his car and headed into the building with the soldier.

Inside the building, he was conducted to a room where maps and printouts of other data covered one of the walls. Tom looked at the maps and recognized some of the points that were highlighted. A few minutes later, the officer in charge of the Green Berets and the mission walked into the room and sat down at the table. He unfolded a map. When Tom looked at it, he saw markings that showed the exact route he, Mark, and Martin had taken on the previous mission. "That is the exact same route," said Tom.

"We spent a lot of time after we spoke with you and Martin locating the entry point into the country," said the officer.

Tom spent about an hour in the room before he was led to a separate room with a bathroom and bed. He needed to be up and ready in the morning by seven o'clock when a soldier would take him to a training area on the base. Tom was able to walk freely around the building. He could tell by the tile on the floor and the ceiling tile that the building had been built many years before. He got on an elevator and headed to the basement where there was a cafeteria. He was surprised at the different types of food available, and he ate a steak with a baked potato. He took his time eating dinner and thinking about the mission. After he was finished, he went back to his room and fell asleep.

The next morning, Tom woke up at six and got ready. He knew the soldier would soon knock on his door. At exactly seven o'clock, there was a knock on the door. Tom opened it and walked with the soldier to a vehicle that was parked in front of the building. From there he traveled to the training site where they were met by the officer in charge of the operation.

Walking into a tented area, Tom was introduced to the three Green

Berets who would go on the mission. They all sat down at a table, and the operation was explained to him in detail. They were to arrive at certain points on the route at certain times, and everything was tied to the clock. The officer in charge had decided to wait until the next night to cross the border. The three Green Berets would be armed, and Tom would be unarmed. They would be using night-vision goggles as they walked the route. Tom thought about the previous mission and the use of flashlights. That was probably the main reason they had been caught. After the operation was explained, the team was instructed to be at the starting point in South Korea by four o'clock the next afternoon. The three soldiers and Tom would be boarding a truck at one o'clock in the afternoon for the drive to the starting point. The drive would take about two hours, so that left an hour of float time.

The next afternoon at one o'clock, a truck approached the front of the building where Tom was staying. He had been waiting, and he got into the truck. The Green Berets were already in the back of the truck. The truck drove through the front gate and traveled north toward the starting point. Arriving at the site at around three o'clock in the afternoon, the team unloaded the back of the truck and walked over to a building that was being guarded. Inside the building was a setup of computers and monitors tied to the satellite positioning system.

Tom had been given camouflage gear at the base, so he was dressed the same as the Green Berets. Inside the building, he was tagged with a signal device for the satellite. It was a small device hidden inside his camo gear. The signal was received on the monitor, so it was checked and was functioning properly. The three soldiers were checking their weapons when the night-vision goggles were distributed to them and to Tom.

As it turned to night, the team loaded into another vehicle and took a ten-minute drive to the starting point. The team got out of the truck and put on their night-vision goggles. Tom was surprised at how well he could see. He had heard about them and seen pictures and movies, but had never worn a pair.

At seven o'clock, the team started out on the marked route. They had to cross a creek on the way to the border and then travel through thick grass and then a wooded area, but the pace was steady, and Tom did not have to stop to catch his breath. At the border, they waited for several minutes while they scanned the North Korean side for soldiers. Everything was clear, and they proceeded to cross the border to the North. It would be another three hours before the team reached the point where Tom had hidden the canister. They were following the route very closely, careful not to deviate from it. This would ensure that they ended up within feet of the canister. The pace slowed some after they crossed the border because they were always on the lookout for North Korean military or police personnel.

Once they arrived at the spot where Tom threw the canister when he was captured, the three Green Berets looked over the area to make sure soldiers were not set up nearby. There was a good chance there would be some type of presence from North Korea in the area, only because they had captured three people in that location. Surprisingly, there was no North Korea military presence.

Tom walked to the area where he knew the canister was located. When he got there, he initially could not spot the canister on the ground, and his heart began to beat faster. His eyes started to jump around as he looked around the area, and he thought that no way the North Koreans had found the canister. After another minute of looking, he pushed some grass and leaves to the side, and there was the canister, hidden. Tom quickly grabbed it and put it inside his inner jacket pocket. He then said over the radio that he had the canister, and the soldiers started to backtrack the way they had come.

The lieutenant in the group of three Green Berets signaled to his commander that they found the package and were returning to the setup point, which was still in North Korea, and they would stay there until night again.

During the hike to the point, Tom heard a sound of a vehicle in the distance. He saw the lieutenant give the signal to stop and find somewhere to hide. Through his night-vision goggles, Tom could make out two military vehicles loaded with soldiers. They were driving along a road approximately a hundred twenty yards away from the team. He believed that, from that distance, they would never be able to spot the team. The military vehicles passed by and disappeared in the distance.

The team resumed their hike for another hour and a half and then set up camp and a perimeter to wait out the day. There was always one of the three Green Berets on point looking for any North Korea activity. The area where they stopped was covered in grass that was five to six feet tall and thick, and a team could easily hide in this brush.

During the day the weather was mild and sunny with temperatures in the midseventies and only a few clouds. They discussed among themselves what had taken place during the mission so far and what was left to do. One of the Green Berets asked, "Tom, what is so important about retrieving the canister? We were never briefed on the contents of the canister."

"The data contains seismic information during an underground nuclear test," explained Tom. "With this information, we can narrow down where earthquakes might happen in the future." Once Tom started talking about the millions of people living along the Ring of Fire, the Green Berets started to nod their heads as if they understood. During the rest of the day, they saw two other vehicles off in the distance, but none came close enough to concerned the team.

When night fell, the team started out on the final leg of the mission to cross into South Korea; they would not be safe until they had crossed the border. If somehow they were captured, the process would be a lot more difficult to get them returned than it had been to return the original team, mainly because they were military soldiers armed with weapons, and the North Koreans would consider this a high threat. As the team approached the border, they began to slow their pace. Tom's heart started to beat a little faster because he knew they were close to crossing.

Once they crossed the border between North and South, the team celebrated, but they still had to hike for a while before they were met by US military soldiers. Boarding a truck, the team took off their night-vision goggles, and for the first time on the mission, they relaxed on the drive back to the base.

Chapter 9

Analysis of North Korea Earthquake Data

At the main office in Seoul, Tom arrived in the morning as he usually did, having stopped off at a drive-through to get a cup of coffee. On this day, he had the recovered earthquake data from the mission. Once he was in his office, Rachel knocked on the door and sat down across from his desk. Tom reached in his pocket and pulled out the flash drive. "Is that the data from North Korea?" asked Rachel.

"Yes, it is, and I just recovered it with a team of Green Berets," he said.

"Did you go on another mission? I've been calling you leaving messages and just assumed you were taking some time off," she said.

"The mission had to be a secret, or I would have told you before it started. Now that it's complete, the military said I could let you know."

"Good thing you didn't tell me, or I would have been worried again, and I don't want to experience that feeling again."

Tom went on to explain the route they took to cross the border and showed her on a map the location where he had hidden the canister. He finished by telling her that three top-notch Green Berets had accompanied him on the mission.

Tom walked out of his office with Rachel and headed to the main room that contained the computer that performed the calculations. He handed the flash drive to Mark, who was surprised to see it again. "Where did you get this?" he said.

"I'll have to tell you about it later, Mark. The most important thing now is to put the data into the computer to see what results are produced," he said. Both Tom and Rachel stood behind Mark as he put the drive into the computer. After a few minutes, the computations started to show up on the screen, and Tom was stunned at what he saw. With this additional information, the calculations of potential earthquakes in five locations increased by 5 percent—from 10 to 15 percent—and the strength increased 0.5 on the Richter scale.

Tom gathered the staff in the room together and told them that Rachel and he would be traveling for the next two weeks to the five locations installing buoy monitoring systems in the ocean. Mark would be in charge while they were gone. He also instructed everyone in the room to calculate what this new data would do to the countries in the location of the earthquakes or tsunamis. The staff started to work on the number crunching, which would take several weeks to perform.

The next morning, Tom picked up Rachel, and they headed to the airport to fly to Tokyo. Before boarding, Tom called Cooper who was the owner operator of the boat they would take when arriving in Makurazaki. "Get the boat ready for tomorrow morning," Tom said. "We'll be there at seven in the morning, and we'll need your boat for four separate trips."

"I was wondering when you'd need my services again," Cooper said. "I'll have it ready to go in the morning."

When they arrived in Tokyo, they took a taxi to a warehouse leased by Tom's office where a truck with a trailer were stored. Also inside the warehouse were buoy monitors to be used to monitor tsunami activity. They would need a forklift to move the monitors into the trailer, so Tom worked on loading the five monitors while Rachel assisted. Tom got into the driver's seat after Rachel finished loading the back of the truck with their travel bags and computers. The trip to Makurazaki from Tokyo would take several hours, and they arrived at the hotel in the city at around eight in the evening. Both of them were tired, so they checked into their rooms and ate a quick meal at the hotel before going to bed.

In the morning, they drove to the pier where Cooper was ready to help them with their equipment. Tom removed one buoy monitor from the trailer and rolled it to the boat where Cooper used a small crane on the boat to lift it aboard. "It's been a while, Cooper! How have you been?" asked Tom.

"I've been fine. The charter boat business hasn't been booming lately," he replied.

"I want to introduce you to Rachel," said Tom.

"Nice to meet you. My name is Cooper."

"Nice to meet you too," replied Rachel.

"Tom, where in the heck are we going today?" Cooper said with a smile.

"I have the coordinates here—roughly three hundred miles from here south of Japan," Tom said. "I figured the boat ride would take most of the day into the evening. Do you agree, Cooper?"

"I agree. We'll arrive at seven or eight o'clock at the latest."

"I figured we'd stay the night on the boat after we deploy the buoy," said Tom.

"We'd better get started then," replied Cooper.

When the boat arrived at the location, there were still several hours of light in the day, so they set the buoy and checked it over to make sure it was functioning. The rest of the evening they talked about things not associated with work. There was one cabin room on the boat, so Rachel took the cabin, and Tom, along with Cooper, slept on the deck.

The next morning at first sunlight, they headed back to Makurazaki. They were going to use the same charter boat for the next three locations, so the next trip, which would be to the location between Japan and China, would take place the next day.

When they arrived at the hotel, Tom asked Rachel, "Where would you like to eat tonight?"

"At a Japanese restaurant of course."

"Sounds good," said Tom. "I'll meet you in the lobby in an hour." Tom headed to his room to get cleaned up from the trip. After taking a shower and getting dressed, Tom took the elevator to the first-floor lobby area where he met Rachel. They took a taxi to the restaurant so they didn't have to drive the pickup with the trailer. At the restaurant, they were seated in a booth. Tom looked around at the restaurant and noticed the many fish tanks positioned in different locations. The lighting was strong enough to read the menus and still provide a romantic setting. "What's good on the menu?" Tom asked Rachel.

"I like the fried rice with shrimp. I try to order that every time I eat at a Japanese restaurant."

"I also like the fried rice with shrimp, but sometimes I add some steak," he said. The waiter showed up at the table, and Tom told him, "Two fried rice meals with shrimp please. I'll have a beer with a glass, and she'll have a glass of wine."

The waiter walked away, and Rachel said, "You just knew I was wanting a glass of wine?"

"I took a shot at it and was right." Tom smiled, and she smiled back at him. The dinner lasted for an hour, and afterwards they made their way back to the hotel to try to get some sleep. "I'll meet you in the lobby at seven," said Tom. "See you in the morning."

The next morning, they boarded the boat and headed off to the second location. The coordinates put the location several hundred miles off the China coast, but that would not stop a wave if a large earthquake occurred. At the location they set the buoy, and everything was functioning and transmitting to the main office in Seoul. "The sun is starting to set. Before it does, I wanted to try my luck at fishing," said Tom.

"I think that's a fun idea," replied Rachel. "Where are the fishing poles, Cooper?"

"I'll get them for you," he said.

After they'd been fishing for about half an hour, Rachel started to pull back on the fishing pole. "I've got something on the line!" she said.

"Start reeling it in!" said Tom. When the fish on the line was pulled up on the boat, it was a large herring, around twleve inches long. "Not bad, Rachel," said Tom.

"I thought it might be bigger because I was really pulling on the rod," she said. Cooper took the fish off the hook and put it back in the water.

When the sun set, Tom put the fishing pole away. "I guess I didn't have much luck fishing. I didn't catch anything! At least you caught something, Rachel."

"It was fun to reel in the fish," she said.

Dinner consisted of some chips and dip along with a sandwich. The ocean was calm, so the boat was steady. The sleeping arrangements were the same as before.

On the trip back the next morning, Tom worked with Cooper to plan the boat trip to Komatsu where they would dock. Cooper was familiar with the port of Komatsu, located on the west side of Japan. This location would be the starting point for the next two trips.

When they arrived at the hotel in Makurazaki, Tom called and made reservations at a hotel in Komatsu for a three-night stay. They would spend the next day traveling from Makurazaki to Komatsu in the boat. After the two trips to install monitors, they would travel back to Makurazaki.

Tom loaded the last two monitors onto the boat, and they headed toward Komatsu. The boat trip took several hours, and upon arriving, Tom and Rachel took a taxi to the hotel. At the hotel, Tom got out his computer and contacted the main office in Seoul. He checked on the work the team was performing and checked on the status of the two monitors they had installed. The two stations were performing fine and sending information to them daily. The team was making good headway on the data and expected to have it finalized in a week. Tom instructed them to keep up the good work; he and Rachel would be back in a week.

The next morning, they embarked on their trip on the boat to the third location between Japan and South Korea in the ocean. The trip would take roughly six hours, so they would get to the point at around two in the afternoon.

When they arrived at the site, the water was choppier than it had been at the other two locations, so it made the installation of the buoy more difficult. The buoy was swinging around on the jib crane and even knocked into Tom. He was knocked to the deck, but he got up uninjured. Once the buoy was positioned, Cooper turned the boat around and headed back to Komatsu. The trip back was bumpy, and after several hours had passed, Tom was starting to feel queasy. He took a Dramamine, and his stomach began to settle. When they got to the port, Tom quickly departed the boat and sat down on the ground for several minutes. Rachel drove Tom back to the hotel, and he went to his room to lie down. He told Rachel that he would call her when he felt better.

After resting for a bit, Tom was up again, and his stomach was fine, along with the motion in his head. He called Rachel. "Rachel, I'm feeling much better now," he said.

"That's good! I thought you were going to throw up when we were on the boat."

"Do you want to have a drink at the hotel bar downstairs?" he said.

"I'll be there in about fifteen minutes."

At the bar, a man approached Tom and sat down at the table. "My name is Chung. I'm a representative of the Chinese government. My position is to monitor earthquake activity in China."

"Nice to meet you, Chung. My name is Tom, and this is Rachel."

"I called your office to try to talk to you, and they told me that you were in Komatsu at this hotel, so I traveled here to talk to you," Chung said. "I wanted to talk to you about earthquake and tsunami information and possibly collaborating."

"It's getting late and we've had a long day," said Tom, "but you are invited to travel with us to the next monitoring site in the morning. The boat ride will give us plenty of time to talk."

"That sounds great," replied Chung. "Where do I need to be in the morning?"

"Show up at the port boat slip number twenty-four at seven o'clock."

In the morning, Tom and Rachel met Chung at the slip, and they boarded the boat. Chung was interested in the buoy monitor, so he looked it over in detail. He asked Tom several questions about the buoy and said that the Chinese government had been developing buoys to deploy off the coast in high-population areas. Now Tom was interested and started to ask Chung questions, telling him about all the monitors located in different countries, but he said that they had been able to able to install only one in Shanghai. He thought that, with cooperation, they might be able to tie the Chinese buoys to his main office in Seoul, increasing the area they could monitor. Chung told Tom that he would talk to his superiors in the government and would let him know if that could take place, adding that the deployment of the buoys was several months from taking place.

Chung then asked Tom why he was setting buoy monitors in the ocean at these particular coordinates. Tom told him about the data retrieved during the underground testing in North Korea. He explained that these locations were determined by their computer modeling to be prime locations for potential earthquakes. He added that, with the data from North Korea, the percentages of probabilities increased some along with the Richter intensity. Chung was surprised that Tom had a computer system that could generate locations and probabilities, and he was surprised that the underground testing had changed the percentages.

Fortunately for Tom, the ocean was stable, and he did not have any motion sickness issues. When they arrived at the location, Chung helped Tom set the buoy into the ocean and anchor it to the ocean floor. When they were sure it was up and running, they returned to Komatsu. On the way back, the discussion turned to the earthquake and tsunami that had happened off the coast of northern Japan. Chung said they were most concerned with the wave that had devastated inland locations. If something similar happened to a city such as Shanghai, there could be many casualties.

When they arrived at the pier, Tom gave Chung his contact information and personal cell number so Chung could call him when he heard from his superiors or wanted to talk about any topics related to the Ring of Fire.

Tom had one more day of traveling from Komatsu to Makurazaki. They would stay one more night in Komatsu and then leave in the morning. Upon arriving in Makurazaki, they loaded their gear into the trailer and started the drive north to the final location off the coast of northern Japan, where the earthquake had occurred. When they arrived in Sendai in the early evening, they checked into the hotel.

Tom had chartered another boat for the trip to the last set of coordinates. As they had before, they would board the boat at seven in the morning and travel to the location. This trip would not take as long as the previous trips. They would have to travel for only three hours back and forth, and they would not need to stay overnight on the boat. They would be back in Sendai before sunset. The deployment of the buoy went well, and they checked it as they had checked the others for proper operation.

The next morning, Tom and Rachel got into their vehicle and headed back to Tokyo where Tom would leave the vehicle with the cargo trailer. They took the items needed for the plane trip back to Seoul and took a taxi to the airport, with plenty of time before the plane departed.

When they were back in Seoul, Tom said to Rachel, "I'll see you at the meeting at the office in the morning. This was a good trip. We accomplished a lot," he added.

"We did get a lot done during this trip. I'm tired," she said, "but I'll be much better in the morning."

The next morning, Tom looked at the monitors, and they showed the new buoy data. He had set up a meeting for eleven that morning to discuss the progress of the team. When discussion at the meeting began, Tom was not surprised to learn the effects predicted for coastal cities. Tom called John at the State Department. "John, this is Tom," he said.

"Nice to talk to you again, Tom. What can I do for you?" replied John.

"I have the numbers now from the data obtained in North Korea. The possibility percentages and the potential strength of earthquakes have both increased some. We have to do something to persuade North Korea to stop underground nuclear testing. Is there any avenue that can be taken to persuade them?"

"Normal channels and diplomatic solutions do not go anywhere," said John. "The only thing that I can suggest is to start the process to have the matter voted on by the United Nations."

"I don't have any idea how to start that process," said Tom. "Can you send me any information on the UN submittal process? I'll have my team review it."

"I'll send you a link to the steps that need to be taken to start the process," said John.

"Thanks, John, this will help a lot. Talk to you again soon." Tom got off the phone with John and consulted with Rachel. After reviewing the information through the link John supplied, they determined that they had several months' work ahead of them before they would have a proposal they could present to the UN. Tom instructed his staff to have the information completed in three months.

Chapter 10

Compiling the Data for the United Nations

The months leading up to the presentation to the UN were intense. The data the computer generated, including coordinates of potential earthquake activity, was reviewed over and over to make sure the information was a hundred percent accurate. Tom supervised as the team put together information on weaker and stronger earthquakes to create a visual of what could take place. The visual presentation took the longest to prepare. It showed the activity and the waves. This presentation would show the five locations and the impact of earthquakes and tsunamis.

The size of the earthquakes and tsunamis would be smaller in this area, so the group worked on presentation of what the Philippines, Japan, Taiwan, and China might expect from this activity. Tom decided to pick only the largest cities for the presentation because there were so many small cities that were next to the ocean. The first part of the presentation showed the effects of an earthquake and tsunami based on data without the North Korean bomb test information. The second presentation factored in the data from North Korea. Out of the five locations, they would narrow it down to three cities per country.

The information they had generated on the wave height and Richter scale were important in accurately showing the effects. Tom instructed the team to use satellite maps of the cities, but they needed more information on the elevations near the shore. Tom sent a team out to gather the additional information they would need at all the city locations so they could finish the visual presentation.

It would take them a full three weeks to compile this work, and after they had the information, it would take another six weeks to input all the data into the modeling system. During this time, Tom had been working with the State Department branch that works closely with the United Nations in Washington. The people at this branch knew how to get presentations on appropriate desks for review. He also notified Kyle in Washington about the conversation he'd had with Chung and the additional data they might gather if they received approval. There was a good relationship between China and the United States, so the Washington officials gave Tom the go-ahead should he be contacted.

The process to have information submitted to the UN and to get nations to vote on it took time. Because it was the United States, the information would first make it to the UN offices for the United States. From there the information would be reviewed by the associates in the office to determine if it should be brought in front of the assembly. The UN ambassador to the United States would then review it with a small group. If it was approved at this level, a formal submittal would be made to the office of the UN. The office of the UN was where all submittals from countries wishing to make presentations or have the assembly vote on resolutions were sent. The procedures were the same for every country—first go to the country's department for approval, then to the UN office.

There was another seismic conference to be held in two weeks, but this one was smaller than the one in Japan. This conference was in Seoul, and Tom was asked by the coordinators to speak about what was being done to anticipate future earthquakes and provide early warning. He agreed, even though he had a lot of work in progress at that time. After the phone call, Tom took some three-by-five cards and wrote talking points on them. His mind turned to Kim, and he wondered if she would be at the conference.

The two weeks went by fast for Tom at the office, with multiple team meetings and visual presentations. The information was slowly coming together. Their target for submitting to the UN was the first week in June. The UN might request additional information, so they had built in several months to revise if needed. Rachel was also going to attend the conference with Tom because they always attended conferences together.

The room at the conference seminar was large enough to seat over one hundred people. The room featured brown carpet and large chandelier lights above. It was a room that could serve as a place for seminars as well as for fancy receptions. As Tom gave his presentation, he looked around the room to see how many were in attendance. He tried to spot any familiar faces, and suddenly he spotted Kim. Rachel had also spotted Kim in the room, but they were unaware that the person sitting next to her was from North Korea also.

At a seminar break, when Tom and Rachel were drinking some refreshment, they noticed the man with Kim in the hallway. Tom assumed this person was from North Korea. He was afraid that the man might be suspicious if he and Rachel approached Kim. Rachel suggested they try to move in closer. Possibly Kim would see them and introduce them to the man.

They worked their way closer until they were within ten feet of Kim. She turned to look at Tom and Rachel, and then she walked up to them. They shook hands, and Kim introduced the man standing next to her. He was another geologist working for North Korea. Tom was relieved at that information, and he knew not to say anything about his time in North Korea. After several minutes, Tom and Rachel made their way back into the seminar room. Tom talked for another hour about the effects ocean waves can have on shoreline cities. Finally, they both headed back to the office.

As it started to get closer to the UN deadline, the team meetings started to get longer, and the topics of discussion were more refined. Tom had reviewed all the information and visuals, which were contained in a bound document that was approximately two inches thick. At the conclusion of the final meeting, Tom addressed the team: "I want to thank you all for the hard work you have put into this project. With this information, I think we have a good shot at getting a resolution passed in the UN."

"I sure hope it passes. I'd really like to see North Korea stop the testing," replied Mark.

Tom had booked a flight with Rachel to Washington DC. They would personally give their proposal to the UN State Department representatives several days before the deadline. When they arrived in Washington, two meetings had already been set up. The first meeting was with the State Department representatives who worked with the United Nations and who would be submitting the proposal. The second meeting was with Kyle to discuss the UN information and any outstanding items, such as working with Chung and China to incorporate their monitors into the computer system in Seoul. The meetings were on separate days so they would not have to rush either one.

The first meeting started at nine in the morning. "In front of you is the information compiled by my team related to the increase in probability of occurrence and increase in severity of earthquakes and tsunamis without the North Korea bomb test data and with the data," said Tom. "This is the information I'm requesting you send to the United Nations. We hope this information encourages the passing of a resolution that will stop North Korean underground nuclear testing."

Tom took the officials through the documents chapter by chapter and answered any questions. "Rachel will now show you the visual presentation we've put together for each of the five locations," he said.

"Before I start, I want to let you know that you are going to be amazed with this visual presentation, because I surely was," said Rachel. The visual presentation really provided a picture of the effects that reading the documents could not. There were not a lot of questions after the visual presentation. At the end of the meeting, the Washington officials said they would submit the information to the United States office of the UN within a week, and they thanked Tom and Rachel.

The next morning, Tom and Rachel arrived at the State Department in Washington and were escorted to a room where Kyle and Tom's superiors were sitting. Kyle and the others got up and shook their hands. "My name is Rachel," Rachel said as she shook Kyle's hand. "It is a pleasure to finally meet you."

"Tom has spoken about you many times," replied Kyle. The group sat down at the conference table, and Tom started the conversation. "This is the earthquake and tsunami data that Rachel and I presented to the State Department representatives yesterday."

"What was your overall impression of the meeting?" asked Kyle.

"I think it went well. They were really impressed with the visual presentation," said Tom.

After they talked about the previous day, the conversation turned to China. Everyone wanted to know if there was any new information. "I have not been contacted by Chung," said Tom. "I do think he will contact me, but I put the odds of allowing him to add their monitors at fifty-fifty."

"Let me know when he does contact you," replied Kyle. From this topic, Kyle turned the conversation to Tom's budget in Seoul. "I wanted to let you know, Tom, that your budget for next year is going to be increased by twenty-five percent."

"Great news!" replied Tom. "I'll definitely put the money to good use purchasing more buoy and land-based monitors."

"I would like you to also add some more staff members," said Kyle.

"We do have a need for additional staff," said Tom.

Tom and Rachel thanked Kyle and the other people present, and they left the State Department.

Tom had built in another float day in case they had to address additional issues during the meetings, so the next day they traveled around to the main attractions in Washington. Rachel had never been to Washington before, so she was excited. They were close to the Washington, Jefferson, and Lincoln memorials, so they visited them first. They then took a taxi to see the White House and the capitol. It took most of the day to see the monuments and attractions, and when they were finished, they headed back to the hotel to relax and change clothes. Their flight was departing at seven the next morning, so they needed to be at the airport by five. After spending some time at the hotel bar, they went back to their rooms and tried to sleep.

Back in Seoul, Tom scheduled a meeting with the team to let them know how the meetings in Washington had gone and to thank them again for their hard work putting the proposal together. Tom explained to his team the process they had gone through at both meetings, and he talked about the questions people had asked.

After a week had passed, Tom got a phone call from one of the Washington UN representatives. He told Tom that the proposal had been submitted to the US office of the UN where it was currently being reviewed. The representatives thought it would go to the next stage within several weeks unless the officials requested additional information.

Tom was more nervous during the coming weeks. After three long weeks, he received another phone call. "Tom, this is Jason with the UN State Department office."

"Yes, Jason. I hope you have some good news!"

"The proposal has made its way up to the US ambassador. At this point, it's just a matter of time before it is approved," he said. "Rarely do documents make it to this stage and then get sent back for revisions," he added.

"This is great news! I'll let my team know right away."

After the phone call, Tom notified Rachel. Then he assembled the team to let them know the great news. "I think we should celebrate! After work, meet me at Mart's and I'll by you all a round of drinks." Mart's was their favorite bar, located a block from the office. After work, the team showed up at the upscale bar to celebrate.

It was another month before the proposal made it to the UN general office, where it would be presented to the assembly of countries. Tom received a call from the US ambassador's office. He was updated on when it would be presented to the other countries. The ambassador's representative asked Tom if he could be at the UN when this took place to answer any questions that might be asked during the assembly. Tom said he and Rachel would book a flight to New York. They would arrive several days before the assembly. He asked how long they would need to stay and was told they should plan on a minimum of one week after the assembly.

It was not uncommon for the countries to ask many questions about resolutions. The resolution the US would propose was to put additional sanctions on North Korea to encourage them to stop underground nuclear testing. Based on the information compiled, the stakes were high. During the month leading up to the presentation, the US officials with the UN were drafting the resolution and had provided the documents and visuals to some of the main Asia countries in the UN. The main countries were Japan, South Korea, North Korea, China, Taiwan, Russia, the Philippines, and Indonesia. All countries were in the Ring of Fire and were in the potential impact area if an earthquake and tsunami developed. Tom and Rachel were available for any questions that might come up during the month.

They answered several questions during this time, most of them well thought out and direct. They even received several questions from Kim Yong-Suk of North Korea. The government had designated her as the person for North Korea related to the resolution. Her questions were about the underground plates along the Ring of Fire; she did not address the nuclear tests. She was trying to create doubt about the information in the documents; specifically, she was trying to disprove the data. Creating doubt about the accuracy of the data was the only thing she could do for the North Korean government. In her mind, she thought the information was accurate, and the nuclear testing was not helping matters. Of course, she would never say anything to her superiors about what she was thinking.

Chapter 11

The Presentation and Decision

Tom and Rachel boarded the plane in Seoul to travel to New York for the presentation and resolution at the United Nations. During the first leg from Seoul to Los Angeles, Tom worked on some last-minute answers to questions. The team in Seoul had gathered the information; it was now a matter of organizing it. This took about three hours. When he was finished they watched the inflight movie. In Los Angeles, they had a two-hour layover before they boarded a plane for the second leg to New York.

During the layover, Tom was on his phone talking to both Seoul and Washington. He was trying to make sure there were no loose ends before the big day in New York. On the plane trip to New York, Tom filled Rachel in on his phone call with Washington.

When the plane landed in New York, it was in the evening. Both travelers were tired and just wanted to check into the hotel and get some sleep.

The next morning, they ate breakfast at the hotel and then took a taxi to the UN headquarters. They had a meeting with the US ambassador at the UN to discuss any last-minute details before the presentation. "All questions that have been submitted have been answered by my team, Miss Ambassador," said Tom.

"Can you see anything that might pop up last minute?" she replied.

"No. I think it has all been covered," he said. The meeting did not take long because the ambassador had a full schedule that day.

Tom and Rachel left UN headquarters and decided to see some of the sights around the city. "Rachel, how about we visit Times Square?" he said.

"I've always wanted to see it, along with Rockefeller Center," she replied.

"The attractions are within walking distance of each other, so let's take a taxi to Times Square first," he said. When Tom got out of the taxi at Times Square, he was amazed at the lighted signs on both sides of the street. "Look at all the signs!" he said to Rachel.

"I know ... it's overwhelming! I bet it looks even better at night," she added.

"There's an Olive Garden in that building," said Tom. "Let's eat there before we leave New York."

"Sounds good, and the government will pick up the tab," replied Rachel.

After walking through Times Square, they walked to Rockefeller Center and took the elevator to the top of the building. Tom looked around and could see all of the tall skyscrapers. He walked into the gift shop and purchased a picture of the building. "What are you going to do with that picture?" said Rachel.

"I'm going to get it framed and hang it on my wall when we get back to Seoul," replied Tom.

After finishing up at Rockefeller Center, they took a taxi back to the hotel. Tom decided they should remain at the hotel for the rest of the night so they could discuss their plans for tomorrow. The presentation would take place the day after tomorrow, so they had a free day to see more sights or do whatever they wanted. Rachel wanted to do some shopping in New York, and Tom wanted to see more sights. He also wanted to ride the subway system in New York to experience it for the first time. Tom would meet up with Rachel later in the afternoon at Times Square. He got on the phone and made reservations at the Olive Garden to make sure they would have a table when they arrived for dinner.

The next day, they split up for most of the day. Tom left the hotel and walked a block to board a subway that would take him to the Freedom Tower. He had watched on television over the years the progress of the tower, and now that it was finished, he wanted to take the elevator to the top.

After visiting the Freedom Tower, he walked several blocks to Wall Street. He took many pictures on his phone of the attractions around New York. He liked Times Square the most, mainly because of the activity that was constantly going on and all the businesses and neon lights.

It was getting close to the time he was to meet Rachel for dinner, so he jumped into a cab and headed toward Times Square.

Tom met Rachel in front of the Olive Garden in Times Square. They walked upstairs to the restaurant. While they ate dinner, Tom had a surprise for Rachel. "What is this?" she asked as he handed her a card in an envelope.

"Open it and find out," he replied.

She opened the card, which read "Thinking of You." Inside were two tickets to *The Lion King.* "Oh my gosh! This is one of the best presents I've ever received!" she said.

"I thought you would like to see a Broadway show before we left New York. I ordered the tickets weeks ago in Seoul," he said.

"Great timing! The show starts in forty-five minutes," she said.

"We're just about finished with dinner, and the theater is only a short walk from here," said Tom.

Tom and Rachel finished dinner at the restaurant and then walked a short distance to watch *The Lion King.* They had a wonderful time and then headed back to the hotel. Tom knew tomorrow was the big day, so they planned to meet in the morning to travel to the United Nations headquarters.

On the morning of the UN presentation, Tom was nervous about the day ahead. He and Rachel arrived at eight o'clock, and they went directly to the United States office. The country ambassadors were assembling in the main room for the meeting, which would start at nine o'clock. Tom and Rachel walked to the main room and were shown where to sit during the assembly. After they settled in, Tom looked around the room. It was enormous with a ceiling that must have been fifty feet tall. The seats for the ambassadors were arranged alphabetically by country and provided the best view of the main assembly podium. From where he was sitting, Tom had a clear view also, but he was on the far left of the hall so he had to turn his head to the right to watch and listen. The ambassadors began to enter and take their seats, and when the assembly was to start, the room was full.

The secretary of the United Nations began speaking about what they would be listening to during the day's events. Not only was the United States going to present a resolution, but representatives from Brazil and Italy would also speak.

The first up to talk about a resolution was the United States. The ambassador spoke about the data that had been put together that explained the relationship between North Korean nuclear testing and earthquakes. The documents Tom and his team had worked on were now in front of all the ambassadors. After the oral presentation, the visual presentation was shown. There were people present from many different countries, and they all spoke different languages, but the video showed everyone what could take place. There was a narrative to go with the visual, and the ambassador did not talk as it was playing.

After the presentation, there were questions from several countries. The ambassador referred all question related to the documents to Tom. The main question asked by several countries was how accurate were his probability percentages and earthquake intensity projections. Tom got up and spoke to the assembly and answered this question by saying the computer program and modeling were state of the art, but without a seismic event occurring close to one of the locations determined by the computer, the data could not be confirmed. The UN assembly would not take a vote on the resolution to impose sanctions on North Korea on that day. They would reconvene in one week to vote, giving everyone time to review the documents. Tom would spend the next week working at the UN office to address any questions.

After the UN meeting, Tom went back to the office in the UN headquarters. He spoke with the ambassador present about the presentation and what the vote might be next week. "I think the presentation went well. What is your take on it, Tom?" asked the ambassador.

"I would definitely agree with your thoughts. The visual presentation pushed everything over the top," he said.

"I was watching some of the ambassadors while it was playing, and I could tell they clearly understood," added Rachel.

"I think we will get a yes vote," said the ambassador.

"We'll be here first thing in the morning," said Tom.

Through the rest of the week in New York, Tom and Rachel, along with their team in Seoul, answered many questions from countries. Tom addressed the main question asked at the assembly but there were other questions, such as how many early-warning sirens had been installed and in what countries they were located.

It was getting toward the end of their stay in New York when Tom got a call from the office in Seoul. There had been a small earthquake close to the location of the large one that had happened off the coast of northern Japan. It was not large, measuring 3.5 on the Richter scale, and the waves that arrived on shore as a result of the quake did not cause any damage. The location was within two miles of the new buoy monitor they had put in place.

When he got off the phone, Tom told Rachel what had occurred. He needed to let the ambassador know that the event had taken place, and specifically that it had occurred close to one of the locations indicated by the computer data.

The next morning, Tom and Rachel sat in the office with the US ambassador while Tom explained to her that a small earthquake had been detected close to one of the locations predicted by the computer. "As you recall, Miss Ambassador, the main question from many countries that I addressed in the assembly was the accuracy of the data generated," said Tom.

"You said that the only way to confirm your data was for an event to occur close to one of the locations," she replied.

"That is correct, and now we have that confirmation. I don't know if you want to let the other nations know that there was confirmation of the accuracy of the data generated," he said. "The knowledge that the data is confirmed might help make a decision."

"I'll send an email to the countries summarizing our conversation," she said.

The vote was to be held the next day, so there was little time for them to send the email. The ambassador hoped most of the ambassadors would read the email.

The next morning, Tom sat in the same location in the assembly hall. The US ambassador walked up to the podium and spoke to the assembly about what had occurred during the week, and specifically about the small earthquake that had occurred and confirmed his team's data. She wanted to make sure that representatives in the room were aware of the events.

After her speech, the assembly had thirty minutes to decide to approve or not approve the resolution. The votes would take place electronically, and the results would show up on a screen. The United States and the other vital nations who had been aware of the contents of the documents in advance were all in agreement to vote yes on the resolution. They knew the importance of limiting underground activity and getting North Korea to stop the testing.

At the end of the thirty minutes, the UN secretary said it was time to vote on the resolution. The votes were—by a large margin—in favor of imposing additional sanctions on North Korea to encourage them to stop the testing. The number of yes votes indicated that the ambassadors had understood the documents and visual presentation. They recognized how important it was to stop the testing. North Korea had already been under sanctions for pursuing the development of nuclear weapons. This resolution overlapped a little on the previous resolution and specifically tried to prevent other countries from helping, such as China, which was the country that provided more help to North Korea than any other. Many nations voiced concerns over imposing sanctions on the country because the people of any country end up suffering from sanctions, but this had to be done to prevent potential earthquakes from happening.

The US ambassador and some of her staff members were going to celebrate, and she invited Tom and Rachel to join them. The celebration, later in the evening, was held at a bar close to the UN headquarters. When Tom walked in the front door, he could tell it was a bar where many diplomats and ambassadors often ate and drank. Inside there were flags from all of the nations represented in the UN. "Plenty of flags in this bar," Tom joked to Rachel.

"There is almost not enough room for all of them," she replied.

"There's the US ambassador," said Tom. "Let's have only a couple drinks and then head back to the hotel."

"We have to get up early to fly back to Seoul, so I agree," replied Rachel.

After a few drinks and conversation with the UN people, Tom and Rachel caught a taxi to the hotel.

The flight back to South Korea was long but uneventful. They arrived in Seoul late in the afternoon and traveled to the office in the morning. At the office, Tom dove into the information obtained from the buoy monitor and looked over the information on the computer. The data the computer developed showed no changes, and Tom was relieved. The locations where they had installed new buoys were the same, and there were no new locations.

At the request of the Japanese government, Tom was asked to provide a further briefing on the latest small earthquake. The government respected his work, even though they had their own team coming up with data. He compiled the information from his team and headed to Tokyo to meet with officials of the government, along with several of the Japanese team that monitored activity. They were concerned about the activity that had occurred off the northeastern coast of Japan; specifically, the most recent small earthquake, and the much larger one a year ago.

By now, the Japanese government had installed many tsunami sirens along the northeastern coast of Japan. Before the large earthquake there had been warning, but officials had determined that more sirens were needed. Tom thought this was a great idea; finally, they were trying to be ahead of any seismic activity. Tom requested information on the locations of the new sirens so he could update his computer system. They compiled the information for him during the meeting, and at the end of the meeting, they gave him the data.

The meeting lasted until early afternoon, so Tom spent the rest of the afternoon at his hotel room studying the locations of the new sirens. The government was adding hundreds of sirens along the coastal cities. The government also installed new tsunami warning devices in the ocean off the coast. They were aware of the buoy monitor Tom had installed, so their tsunami stations were closer to the shore. Tom suggested they somehow tie that buoy to the new tsunami buoys closer to shore and the new sirens. This would create a series, so if the outer monitor detected something, it would signal the buoys closer to the shore. Depending on data, sirens could be activated to warn of a tsunami.

That evening, Tom flew back to Seoul with the additional information, and several weeks later, he got a call from Tokyo agreeing to tie his station together with their stations. Tom provided them with the data they needed and asked them to send his team the information on the tsunami buoys and sirens when they were complete and running.

There was more work to do to increase the safety factor for everyone along the Ring of Fire. Tom would work with John to try to get the countries that had installed only minimal tsunami warning systems to add to their systems as Japan had done. South Korea, China, Russia, and Taiwan agreed to add monitors and sirens, but the Philippines, Indonesia, and

Vietnam were more reluctant, mainly because of the cost. However, some of the countries along the Ring of Fire provided funds to these countries so additional buoys and sirens could be installed.

Despite the sanctions imposed on North Korea, the other countries also provided the equipment and expertise to install monitors and buoys off their shoreline.

Chapter 12

North Korea's Response

The leader of North Korea wanted the documents his country had obtained during the UN meeting analyzed further, so they were sent through channels to Kim Yong-Suk. She had a small team working with her in the government. She immediately started working on the documents, first reading through them, then separating data for further analysis. She would use the information obtained during the underground testing in her research.

She had already reviewed the documents that were a part of the UN resolution, but this time she and her team were going to dissect the data further. There were currently no monitors installed in the country, so additional data in North Korea would be impossible to gather. The data weighed heavily on the effect of the testing, and from their analysis, it was difficult to disprove the information from Tom's team: when the test was performed, the number on the Richter scale was relatively the same, and the shaking of the ground only complicated and increased the probability of a future earthquake. Through the conferences she had attended, she was aware of the correlation between fracking in the United States and earthquakes. If earthquakes were happening just by drilling and fracking, then a detonation underground might have the same effect.

Many months passed before Kim and her team completed a proposal. The information put together would make its way up the chain of command. In her report, she did recommend stopping the underground testing, but she knew in her mind this would not happen. The activities of the North Korean military took precedence over anything else.

Another two months passed before she got a call from General Hanbin. He wanted to meet her at his office to discuss her information further.

On the day of the meeting, she traveled to the military office in Pyongyang. Kim walked into the general's office and sat down in front of his desk. She looked around the room and saw many pictures of the general with other officers and with the leader of the country. A case on the wall held his promotions and military decorations. "Now that you have had time to review the information from the UN, what did you find?" he said.

"The data is accurate with regard to increased probability and increased strength," she said.

"They can't possibly think that our underground nuclear tests could contribute to an increase in seismic activity," he said.

"There is no possible way that can be proved," she said. "Nobody knows with a hundred percent accuracy where or when an earthquake or a tsunami might occur, but if you want my professional opinion, the underground tests need to stop. They know that any activity under the ground, and especially of the magnitude of nuclear explosions, only increases the chance," she added.

"If the sanctions imposed on this country were lifted, and trade was started again with North Korea and the other Asian countries, I think that would certainly end the underground tests," he said.

"I also think the sanctions should be lifted," she said. Before she left the office, the general told her that they were getting equipment and expertise to install buoy and land-based monitors. Kim was excited that new, up-to-date equipment would be arriving in North Korea.

The equipment arrived at the government warehouse in Pyongyang. Kim was present when it was unloaded—a total of four buoys and five land-based monitors. Kim met Jeff from Tom's office who was familiar with setting up the equipment. Before his arrival, Kim worked with her team to determine where they would install the monitors. She had arranged for a boat to take them along the shoreline, and she had arranged for trucks and personnel to drive to the land-based locations.

Kim traveled to parts of North Korea with Jeff, watching him set up the land-based monitors. As they were set up, Kim and another man from her office were shown how to check them to make sure they were functioning correctly. Included with the equipment were four laptops loaded with the monitoring programs. The monitors could communicate via a satellite, but in this case, a small antenna was set up so it would send signals to a main antenna at Kim's office in Pyongyang. There might be a satellite connection possible in the future.

Once the five locations were set up, they traveled back to Pyongyang to set up the main antenna on the government building and then run the cable through the building to their office. The installation of the cable from the roof to the office took some time because the building was made of concrete.

When the laptops were hooked to the wires, they received the data from the five monitors. Two of monitors had not been supplied by South Korea, but had been picked up during the mission Tom was on when he was captured. The monitors had been turned over to Kim by the military. These monitors were more compact, and Kim had decided the best place to install them was at the location where they had been removed.

With the help of the military, Kim drove to the location close to the underground testing and installed the monitors at that location. These monitors did not have antennas because they were going to send a signal through a satellite. Kim was able to find two antennas in North Korea and set them up at the location. They did not have to be ordered because the antenna was to only send a simple signal, like a television antenna. Upon returning to Pyongyang, Kim watched as the signal was detected at the main office.

The next trip would be to the boat to install the buoys in the ocean. She would make two trips back and forth, helping Jeff install the two buoys, one each day. The days were long, and they didn't arrive back at the dock until late in the evening. The buoys were installed in locations where there was the largest concentration of population along the shore. These were the people who would be most at risk.

Back at her main office, her team checked the monitors and the computer program to make sure no issues were detected before Jeff left North Korea the next day. He would spend most of the day training Kim and her team on the computer software. This program had many different streams of data.

The next morning, a car arrived to take Jeff back through the border. Kim was present, and she thanked Jeff for his work in helping set up the monitors. As Jeff drove away, Kim turned to one of her friends in the office and said that this project would be a tremendous help for North Korea.

Over the next several months, the monitoring system detected small tremors in different locations along the Ring of Fire, but nothing that was concerning. The recordings of the tremors were analyzed just as recordings of larger earthquakes would be analyzed. The office environment was normal, with no overtime spent, and the team was more relaxed. It was a long time between the vote for additional sanctions and an official response from North Korea.

Tom was watching television in the office when the breaking news appeared on the screen. It was the response to the United Nations resolution originating from Pyongyang. The response was what Tom was expecting—the North Korean leader said they would continue to develop their nuclear program, and the additional resolution only made them more resolved. He said they welcomed dialogue among other countries, including the United States. Adding to that, he also said that, if the sanctions were lifted, then they would consider halting the nuclear program, but he did not give specifics. At the end of his speech, he said he and his administration needed to protect their people and North Korea.

Tom shook his head, knowing they were not making any changes that would help the Ring of Fire, but he was encouraged that the leader was open to dialogue. He thought South Korea should be the first country to contact North Korea. Tom called John to talk to him about the news. "John, I'm sure you've heard the response from North Korea, and I wanted to talk to you about the current situation."

"I just saw it on television," he said. "What specific issue do you want to discuss?"

"I think you should start rattling the trees with some of your superiors and the South Korean government. This is a perfect opportunity to establish better relations with the North."

"I agree with that statement, but I don't have that kind of influence. It is a South Korean matter. I'll tell you what I can do. I can call a friend in the South Korean government and relay your thoughts."

"Anything you can do, John, would help. Thank you for doing this for me." Tom finished the phone call.

When John called his friend, the entire phone call was narrowed down to one response by him. It would be some time before a decision would be made about dialogue. John called Tom to let him know he'd had a conversation with a South Korean diplomat, and he relayed the diplomat's response. The approval to contact North Korea would have to be made by the president of South Korea. There were also people in the South Korean government who were against any contact with North Korea, so the matter was strictly political at this point.

The routine at Tom's office was normal. Every year the team gathered data from the monitors and often traveled to physically check them. There was no indication in any of the readings that would indicate that North Korea was resuming their underground testing.

Tom decided it would be a good time to send his request in for a two-week vacation, and he asked Rachel if she would accompany him to the States. She thought it would be wonderful and made plans to leave with him.

When the day arrived to start their vacation, Tom and Rachel boarded a plane and flew to Los Angeles. From Los Angeles, they flew to Las Vegas and checked into Caesar's Palace. Together, they took in the sights in Las Vegas and watched several shows. They also gambled some.

Leaving Las Vegas, Tom drove a rental car to the Grand Canyon where they took a raft down the Colorado River. Even though he was on vacation, he called the office daily to check in. Finishing the trip to the Grand Canyon, Tom drove back to Las Vegas. He had planned to drive from Las Vegas to Los Angeles, so they left Las Vegas three days before the flight back to Seoul.

They arrived in Los Angeles and traveled to some of the attractions—the Hollywood Walk of Fame and Rodeo Drive. Their hotel was close to the beach, so they spent a day soaking up the sun. It was during this time in Los Angeles that Tom was starting to feel different about Rachel. Instead of seeing her strictly as a professional colleague, he started to have feelings of love for her. He did not say anything to Rachel about his feelings; he kept them to himself. There were things to sort through in his mind; the main issue was how this would affect their work.

The morning of the plane flight to Seoul, they arrived at the airport with plenty of time to pick up some tourist items for Mark and the staff. Arriving back in Seoul, they both went to their homes. Tom would spend another day resting and getting things in order around his house.

It was getting later in the year, and there had been several small tremors detected throughout the Ring of Fire. The area where the large earthquake and tsunami had occurred in northern Japan was still active with small tremors. When activity was recorded, Tom's team would always contact Japan officials to discuss and verify the data. The data would always match, so it was another verification of the computer program working correctly.

During the last month of the year, the monitors in South Korea indicated that a new earthquake had occurred. The monitors in the northern part of South Korea indicated a Richter scale number about the same as the reading obtained when an underground test occurred. Tom was quickly alerted in his office, and he walked out to the control room. Looking at the computer, he saw that the buoy in the ocean indicated a seismic event. Tom did a little more calculating and determined another nuclear test had occurred in North Korea.

Tom asked his group to research even further and document the event. They started to work on the information to determine with a hundred percent accuracy that the underground test had happened. No television station in North Korea announced a new test, and Tom thought the UN resolution had made the country more secretive. His thinking turned to how easy it would be to get reliable feedback if he could call Kim on the mobile phone to discuss their data and find out if a test occurred. Maybe in the future, his office and their office would collaborate on earthquake data.

Chapter 13

More Nuclear Testing

Kim knew through talking with people at the underground test site that each test was advancing North Korea's nuclear program. Each underground test was working the way they wanted it to work. Through Kim's work, they were aware that the testing could be causing underground instability, but they thought it was minimal and nothing to be concerned about. Their intent was to develop nuclear weapons and become a nuclear country like the United States and Russia. Kim was to be present for the every future test. There would be a total of two more tests, excluding the test last week.

When Kim drove around Pyongyang, she could tell that the sanctions really were not doing much good, and North Korea was operating normally. The United States had been trying for years to get China to help them along with other countries in the United Nations. China tried diplomatically to get North Korea to abandon their program, but North Korea continued. The relationship between China and North Korea was solid, and China did not want to do anything more than ask them to stop.

Kim Yong-Suk was standing outside her office when a car arrived to pick her up. "I'm your driver, and I'll be taking you to the test site," he said.

"I was not told of a new test," she said. "I was told only to show up here at a specific time. I can tell the underground tests have become more secretive."

"I was only informed an hour ago to pick you up," he said.

Kim wanted to tell the driver why she thought the tests had been more secretive, but she did not know what level security clearance he had. When she arrived at the site, a general took her aside and informed her that only one more test was going to take place after this one. The underground test was scheduled for the afternoon. She felt relief that they were going to stop the testing. She thought that, after the testing stopped, the area around the Ring of Fire would be safer.

When she got to the site, she set up her equipment as she had done before. "This test will be a smaller detonation than the previous tests," said a technician.

"Thanks for letting me know," she replied. "Without that information, I would be wondering why the reading was lower than readings in previous tests."

The underground test occurred at two in the afternoon. The ground shook as it had before, but it was difficult to determine if the ground shook less than before. Kim could only determine this information by looking at the data. The data showed that the earthquake was smaller by a factor of 0.8 on the Richter scale.

After the celebration at the main building and before Kim got into a car for the drive back, a general told her that the last test would occur in the next month, and she would be contacted. She wished she could contact Tom and let him know there was only one more test. There were no conferences before the last test, but there was one later in the year, so she might be able to tell him then.

Tom was in the main control room when the monitors along the North Korean border picked up the seismic activity, and the results were calculated in Seoul. This had been the second time in a month that another underground test had been performed. The activity was not as strong as it had been in the past tests, so Tom thought this was a smaller detonation. Tom got on the phone and called John to discuss the matter. John was unaware of the test, so he was interested in the results Tom and his team had calculated. Tom told John that the data indicated a smaller quake occurring in North Korea. Tom wanted John to contact the officials in the South Korean government to let them know that the event had taken place. He wanted John to try to put more pressure on the South Korean government to hold talks with the North. As it had been with the previous test, North Korean officials did not announce the test after it was completed.

Tom had a meeting with John and the official from South Korea to discuss the events. The three men determined that the UN resolution was the reason the North Koreans were keeping the ongoing underground testing secret for now. Tom told the others that, despite the fact that the testing was supposed to be secret, his data clearly proved the underground testing. Tom told John that he was going to speak with Washington about the latest test.

"Kyle, this is Tom. How are you doing?"

"I'm well. How about yourself?"

"I'm fine, but I'd be a lot better if North Korea would stop their underground tests," he said.

"I saw in an email that another test took place," replied Kyle.

"Yes. They're trying to keep it a secret, but I have the data from the monitor that's up close to their border."

"You need to put some pressure on the UN. I suggest getting the North Korean ambassador in a meeting and exposing the latest test," said Tom.

"It will be tough, but I'll call the US ambassador and try to persuade her to have that meeting."

"Great! Let me know the details of the meeting if it takes place. Thanks for your help and support, Kyle."

After the phone call, Tom decided to leave early from the office to take care of some things he'd been neglecting at home. Before he left, he searched until he found Rachel. "Rachel, I'm going to leave early this afternoon, but I wanted to let you know the status of my phone call with Kyle."

"I was wondering how it went. Fill me in on the details," she said.

"Kyle is going to contact the US ambassador and try to get a meeting with the North Korean ambassador. During the meeting, the continual underground testing will be addressed. I asked him to let me know when he finds out information on the meeting."

"I know you'll let me know as soon as that happens," said Rachel.

"You know I will," replied Tom.

The meeting with the ambassador of North Korea was short and to the point. The US officials presented the data Tom and his team had obtained that proved the testing. The ambassador denied they were testing and said the data could have been an earthquake—a natural occurrence. He ended the conversation by saying he would pass this information along to his superiors in North Korea.

Several weeks passed before one of the new monitors Tom and his team had installed in the ocean picked up some activity between Japan and South Korea. It was not a large event, only enough to set the monitors off. Usually when a monitor showed activity, Tom and Rachel would travel to the monitor to visually check it over for any problems.

This time was different; Tom packed his bags and headed alone to Makurazaki. He contacted Cooper, who prepared his boat, and they traveled the same route as before.

When they arrived at the buoy monitor, Tom checked the equipment over and found no signs of damage.

When they arrived back in the city, Tom had a message on his phone from Mark at the office asking Tom call him because there had been another test in North Korea. Tom called Mark to get the details of the event. This had been a smaller seismic event, just like the previous one. Tom told Mark he would be back at the office the next day. He was eager to get back to the main office, but his flight back to Seoul would not be until the morning.

In North Korea, Kim Yong-Suk took a vehicle to the test site where the next test was scheduled, just as she had done before. Her thoughts were about this test being the last underground test. When she arrived at the site, she saw fewer military personnel than she'd seen for the prior tests, but still some high-ranking officers. The leader of the country arrived, and the test was performed. Kim recorded data. After the explosion, the room was silent. There were no cheers and handshakes as there had been after the other tests. She thought the last underground test would be more celebrated by everyone.

In Pyongyang, she would focus the team's attention on the monitors and buoys in North Korea. As she had with the previous tests, she gathered the data from the new monitors and put it into the computer program. There was plenty of data from these monitors, and a lot more items for her team to work on. With the monitors spread out around the country, the data was different from each location. She had another meeting with the same general in Pyongyang in a week, so she wanted to have all the data compiled for him.

During the week, she and her team calculated the data from the different locations, taking into consideration the correlation between distance and depth. The report was going to be as simple as possible because the general did not have much knowledge about earthquakes and tsunamis. With the information, Kim was able to simplify her report to one sheet of paper, front and back. On one side, she listed all the Richter readings from the monitors, and on the other side she outlined the probability of earthquake activity at the locations.

"Hello, General. It is good to see you again," said Kim.

"Nice to talk to you again also," he said.

"This is the information from the newly installed monitors located around the country." Kim handed the general the one-sheet report. "On one side is the Richter scale readings or the strength of the seismic activity. On the other side are the probabilities a seismic event such as an earthquake would occur in each area."

"I like this," replied the general. "I don't know a lot about this subject, and this report is simple," he added. "I'll look over this information in more detail and call you if I have any questions. You must excuse me. I have another meeting in another part of the building, and I must leave."

"Thank You for your time, General," said Kim. She left the building and returned to her office.

Tom followed the same protocol he'd followed before and called Washington with the data that indicated that a seismic event had occurred in North Korea. By now there was nothing much they could do to prevent more tests. Sanctions and meetings were not doing the job. North Korea was moving ahead to advance nuclear ambitions. The president of the United States had been briefed on the underground testing and earthquake activity. Tom informed Kyle he had been trying to get John to put a little pressure on South Korea to open talks with the North, but it had not gone far. Kyle in Washington cautioned Tom from getting involved with those matters and stressed there were people in Washington talking to South Korean officials daily. Tom thought that the data that he and his team had compiled would have more impact than generalities during the US talks with South Korea.

Weeks went by with little change in the stance of South and North Korea in relationship to talks. There were no earthquake events during this time, and Tom thought it was a good time to send out the teams again to check the monitors. The teams were put together the same as before, and they all went in different directions. Tom and Rachel headed out to Japan as before and traveled to the same locations.

During their time in Japan, Tom got a call from Chung. Chung let him know China had finished installing their monitors and buoys and they were willing to let Tom and his team add these monitors to their monitoring system. Chung asked Tom if he was in Seoul, and Tom told him they were in Japan and would be there for a week. Surprising Tom, Chung said he could meet him in Japan in two days with the coordinates and signals for their newly installed monitors. Tom told Chung that, in two days, they would be in Tokyo, where they could meet at their hotel.

When the day arrived, Tom met Chung in the bar area of the hotel. Chung had the coordinates of the monitor sites along with the signal frequencies Tom needed to input the new equipment into his computer system and tie to the satellite system. The meeting lasted several hours, and Chung asked Tom to keep him in the loop if any new information came from the entire monitoring system. Tom said he would certainly let him know any new information or changes. Tom and Rachel would have two more days in Japan, traveling to the final monitoring site off the northeast coast of Japan.

When they left Tokyo, Tom drove them to the location of the final monitor. After they checked the monitor and returned to shore, Tom decided to drive farther north along the coast. Because it was late in the day, they could go only so far before they had to turn around and head back to the hotel. Tom had mainly been looking to see how much the cities along the affected area had been able to rebuild from the earthquake and tsunami. From what they saw, the areas affected had been rebuilt and showed almost no signs that an earthquake and tsunami had occurred. He was also able to see some of the new warning sirens that had been installed to warn of future tsunami events.

The next morning, when Tom and Rachel were about forty-five minutes out of the city Sendai on their way home, they received a call from Mark at the main office. An earthquake had occurred on the island of Kyushu in southern Japan.

Chapter 14

New Earthquake along the Ring of Fire in the Ocean

Tom had not anticipated staying longer in Japan, but now with news of the earthquake on the island of Kyushu, he planned to head back to Seoul that afternoon and then turn around and travel back to Japan in a day's time. Tom asked one of the team members in Seoul to book tickets on the next flight back to Tokyo in the morning for him and Rachel.

When they arrived in Seoul, there was enough time for both of them to get to the office and gather as much information as possible before flying back to Japan.

At the office, Mark told Tom it had been determined that the earthquake measured 7.0 on the Richter scale, which made it a midsized quake. It was smaller in magnitude than the 9.0 quake that had occurred, but large enough to shake the ground. It was located close to the Kumamoto Prefecture on the island of Kyushu. Tom made arrangements to stay at a hotel located within driving distance of the areas affected.

Tom and Rachel left Seoul the next morning, and upon arriving in Tokyo, picked up the truck with the trailer and drove to the hotel. Tom had contacted officials in the Japanese government to let them know they were arriving in Japan and were staying in the city of Fukuoka. At the hotel, they checked in and then each grabbed a bag before driving farther south.

By the afternoon, the team Tom wanted to be onsite had also landed in Japan; it would take them several hours to make the drive south.

When the team arrived at the hotel Tom had booked for them, they called Tom to determine what they needed to do next. At Fukuoka, Tom set off to drive to different parts of the island with Rachel to decide if there was any structural damage and if the earthquake caused a tsunami.

Some of the buildings were destroyed, and there had been casualties in the areas. When the team arrived and joined Tom, he instructed them to drive farther south and analyze data and gather information. The earthquake had not generated a tsunami wave, so that data did not need to be determined. While they were assessing any damage, Tom would stop at the tallest buildings and make visual assessments of the structures.

Tom coordinated with the Japanese officials and collaborated with them to learn their findings. For the rest of the day, they would travel to as many cities as they could, checking out the structures for damage. Some areas had been hard hit with damage; the people would need quite some time to rebuild. The Japanese officials were performing some of the same analyses Tom was carrying out.

The next morning, Tom's team members continued to assess the damage done by the earthquake, traveling to as many towns as possible. Tom spent the late afternoon with the team members in the hotel conference room looking over the data. As they discussed the data, one of the team members input items of significance into a computer for further analysis in Seoul. When it was past eleven that night, Tom told his team to get some sleep because they needed to be at the airport early in the morning.

The plane took off at eleven and arrived safely in Seoul. At the office, as the data was input into the main computer program, Tom watched the probabilities to determine if there were any more locations to be concerned about and. "I think the computer data I'm reading indicates that we need to install another monitor," said Tom.

"I'm reading the same thing," replied Mark.

"What do you think, Rachel?" said Tom.

"I'm in agreement with you two," she said.

"I need to get on the phone to have the team check monitors in the Philippines and install a new monitor in Kyushu," he said.

The information again pointed at the underground testing, and they compiled the information as they had done before and put it into a format that could be sent to Washington. Kyle wanted the information, as did the US ambassador to the United Nations. Another resolution was not going to be put together for this information, but they did want to share the information with the other countries. Tom had copies made for South Korea as well as Japan, because of their close working relationship.

The information obtained with the data would enforce what the computer put together, so Tom wanted his team to focus on the areas being monitored in the oceans. As the year was ending, there was more activity with the volcano located in the Philippines. This added activity prompted Tom to take a trip to the location for further analysis. He was cutting the trip tight because he had to be in Taiwan for another conference the next week.

When Tom arrived in the Philippines and traveled to the site, the volcano erupted, emitting a plume of smoke that was large enough to cause aircraft to be rerouted around the volcano. The monitors were showing an increase in activity, but it was a small increase and was only due to the volcanic activity. The most interesting thought Tom had was that maybe this activity was helping relieve the plate stresses far below the ground. It was only a thought in his mind, a thought that could not be confirmed. Some of the residents living around the volcano had moved to new locations during the event, but some had decided to stay. There were no indications that the volcano would erupt in a manner that might cause devastation to the area, such as blowing out the side of the mountain as in the case of Mount St. Helens in Washington State in the United States. While Tom was there close to the volcano, he could feel minor shaking under his feet.

Leaving the Philippines, he traveled to Taiwan to attend the Conference of Asia Nations. He did not have to speak at the conference as he had in the past, so he relaxed some and walked around the booths and attended a few seminars. Rachel did not attend this conference; rather, she stayed in Seoul, working at the office.

While walking around to the booths, Tom ran into Kim Yong-Suk from North Korea. "Hello, Kim," he said. "It's good to see you at another conference. How are those monitors working in your country?"

"The monitors are working great. I'm not supposed to say anything, but the last underground test helped us better understand the monitors and how they worked."

"We picked up the seismic activity and determined that you had another test," he said.

"Yes, but it was our last underground test. I bet you are happy to hear that, because I was very happy when I knew it was the last test."

"That is wonderful news, Kim."

"Please do not tell anyone related to the South Korean government, because I don't want someone speaking to the North and finding out I told you this."

"I promise that I won't discuss it with them. Have a good time at the conference," said Tom. He walked on to view more booths, and Kim did the same.

The next day at the conference, Tom ran into Chung from China. Their conversation involved the sharing of the Chinese monitors with Tom and his team. Tom also shared information that his team had gathered on the last larger earthquake in southern Japan. He happened to have the documentation his team put together, and he told Chung he would meet him later to give it to him. After the conference ended for the day, Tom met Chung and handed over the documents.

During the plane trip back to Seoul, Tom wrote down the names of the individuals he would notify about the testing in North Korea. First on the list was Rachel, and then Mark in the office. He would also notify Kyle in

Washington. He decided not to let John know because he was concerned this information would make its way to officials with South Korea, and that might make its way to the North. Kim had provided sensitive information to Tom over the years, and he did not want her caught.

Several weeks later, there was word from Pyongyang. The North Korean leader let the rest of the world know they had stopped the underground testing. It was a surprise to some that he would let that information out of the country, and there was no communication at the time between North Korea and South Korea. The leader had reversed his original stance on underground testing, taking the first step to negotiations with the South. Tom was very relieved because this would ensure Kim Yong-Suk would not be exposed.

There would be additional help from Chung and China when they convinced North Korea to include the monitors set up in the country and in the ocean to be added to their system of monitors so they could track their activity. They did not say anything to them in the beginning about their cooperation with South Korea related to monitoring, but this would eventually be addressed. North Korea would not have any issues with the information being shared amongst the countries along the Ring of Fire.

Their cooperation with the other countries, especially South Korea, was a surprising turn of events after their announcement to stop underground testing. This was the first time all the countries around the Ring of Fire had been constructive in communicating with each other.

Even though the Chinese had brokered an agreement about tying their monitors together, the upper military command asked Kim Yong-Suk to contact Tom in South Korea to find out if Jeff was available again to travel to the North. They were aware of the satellite that was tied to the monitors and the main computer, and knew they were picking up their monitors through China, but they wanted a direct link also. Tom arranged with Kim to send Jeff to perform the needed programming.

Once they were online and communicating with the office in Seoul, there was a total of thirty-five monitors located in and around the countries. It was at this point that Tom thought that his system was ready to communicate with the other countries. Approval to do this would have to be made in Washington, but if the sharing approved, the countries in the region would be able to get up-to-the-minute information from Seoul. It was important to receive this information quickly because minutes would save lives if a tsunami was approaching the shores of any of those countries.

The approval to start installing the programs in each of the capitals of the Asian countries was given several weeks later by the secretary of state.

Tom started to call the head geologists working for the governments of the countries that would have the program. He was friends with many of the them through his work in Seoul. Getting them to accept the installation of this system was not hard. Of the all geologists he called, not one of them turned him down.

The next step was for Tom and Rachel to travel to the capitals with four team members who were very familiar with the programming. They split the group up into two teams, with Tom and Rachel each in charge of two team programmers. Tom would travel to Tokyo, Pyongyang, and Taipei, while Rachel would travel to Jakarta, Manila, Beijing, and Hanoi. They were each going to spend two days in each capital, spending the first day traveling and starting to install the program, and the next day finishing installation and running the system to make sure there were no problems.

As was the case on previous trips to check on monitors, they would have an official there to act as an interpreter and make sure things ran smoothly. Both Tom and Rachel experienced success at each of the locations they traveled to. In each location, not only did they install the program and get it up and running, but they also wired the system to an external alarm. The alarm would sound if an earthquake was detected, giving an audible sound like a fire alarm system. It would be loud, but not so loud that people would be putting their hands over their ears. This would ensure someone would know that something was happening even if they were not working on the program or looking at television monitors at the time.

The complete system was online and monitoring for any potential earthquakes. Both teams flew back to Seoul, and at the main office, Tom could look at the screens and see the monitors as before, but also the locations of the capitals on the screen and the status of the system at those locations. Tom quickly put together a small celebration, complete with cake and drinks, to celebrate the completion of the program install. That night, Tom slept better than he had any night in the past several years. Knowing the system was online and running was all he thought about as he drifted off to sleep.

After everything was online, Tom scheduled a conference call every two weeks between the officials at each capital. The call to each country would last only thirty minutes, so he could get all the phone calls in on one day. Rachel would sit in on the conversations and add any questions she might have. Tom also made sure one of the team members who had helped in the installation would be present.

Tom wanted to do more to thank his team for their work, so he scheduled an evening party to celebrate. There was some money remaining in the budget that he could spend on this party, so he first talked to Rachel, and she agreed to help. He didn't need to contact Washington for approval because it was in his budget, and he determined where the money could be spent.

On the night of the party, Tom arrived at a restaurant bar called Ming's located in the business district of Seoul. He wanted to make sure the private room was set up along with the food he had ordered. He looked around the private room at the metal-siding walls and the black carpet. There was a large table in the center where the food would be placed. Rachel was the second person to arrive. "Tom, is everything ready for the party?" she asked.

"I've checked with the wait staff, and the food will be brought in shortly," he said.

The other members of Tom's team showed up a few minutes later. Mark turned to Tom. "Good thing we're on the first floor in case the room starts shaking." Tom laughed at the earthquake joke. Everyone at the party had a great time eating and drinking, and it lasted till midnight. Most of the team had taken taxicabs so they wouldn't have to drive home when they'd had too much to drink. Tom had scheduled the celebration on a Friday so people wouldn't have to worry about getting up and going to work the next morning.

Chapter 15

North and South Korea Start Negotiations

The initial cooperation between North Korea and the rest of the Asian countries was only the beginning. Simply setting up earthquake monitors around North Korea and then eventually linking them to the rest of the monitors had started something. Tom had a good feeling about the direction North Korea was taking. He thought this could lead to something larger. In a conversation Tom had with John, they shared a sense of cooperation that John said the South Korea government had noticed.

Suddenly, for the South Korean government. the idea of contacting North Korea was beginning to be more important. At no time in the history between North and South Korea had there been more cooperation from North Korea. South Korea had set up a meeting between their president and diplomats in their government to discuss how and when to contact the North. Tom was asked by the South Korean government to attend the high-level meeting. The government officials knew the importance of his position and they admired his determination during the UN resolution.

At the meeting, Tom just sat at the table and listened to the South Koreans talk about contacting the North. He had some ideas, but he did not say anything because this was between the South and the North. The current sanctions on the North was a big topic to discuss. To get any of those sanctions changed or lifted would require a United Nations vote. During the meeting, it was agreed that they would take small steps during the initial contact. They would offer any technical and professional services in agriculture and municipal work. It did not seem like much, but it was a good starting point for further conversations. The meeting ended with the South Korean officials deciding they would contact the North a week from Wednesday.

Tom thought that, technically, the decision might be skirting along the boundaries of the UN resolution, but they should not allow the wording of the resolution to hold back their progress. To actually be out of compliance they would have to do something like sell North Korea oil or provide them money.

The following week, Tom was present when the South Korean negotiators gathered at Panmunjom. Inside the old building constructed after the end of the Korean War there was a two-way communication system with the North. Several days before, they had contacted the North to let them know negotiators with South Korea would be present on Wednesday to discuss matters with the North. They wanted to make sure the North had negotiators present during the communication.

On Wednesday morning, the South Korean officials contacted the North at nine in the morning, and the conversation lasted about an hour, during which time South Korean officials offered some of their services. During the conversation, the North did not initially accept their offers, but said they would relay the information to their leader. At the end of the conversation, the two sides set up another day in several weeks to communicate again. Tom was impressed by the way the negotiators from the South and North smoothly talked to each other. He had never been a part of high-level negotiations; he had only picked up his information from watching television.

For the next two weeks, Tom worked at the office monitoring the Ring of Fire. There was nothing to analyze because everything in the area was stable. There were always monthly reports to fill out because his team was part of the State Department, so Tom spent time on these reports. The reports had to do with budgets and employee evaluations; they summarized the team's work for the month. Once he finished with the reports, he would send them to Kyle in Washington.

The two weeks between communications between the North and South seemed to move quickly, and Tom was anxiously waiting for the next conversation.

The second conversation with the North started with the North accepting the South's offer for support. They were particularly interested in the agriculture expertise they could offer. Tom stood in the back of the room but could clearly hear the conversation. This was an important topic for North Korea because they wanted to make sure their crops were producing the maximum yield and could easily feed the population. The North representatives briefly touched on the winter Olympics that were going to be held in South Korea. Not much was said during this communication, only a brief reference to the games. At the end of the conversation, another day and time was set up for further talks. They would hammer out the details on the technical and professional services.

A team of experts in agriculture was assembled to travel to the North. Included were three members from South Korea and two members from the United States. John, from the State Department, was given the task of picking the US members, and he relied heavily on Washington experts to find two of the best in this field.

John was present at the third meeting when it was determined that the agricultural team would travel North on a Monday one month from the conversation. The two US team members made arrangements to be in Seoul a week before they would travel north. During the week leading up to the meeting, they would compile information on the crops and food grown in the North along with information about any new chemicals that were available. The two US team members already were educated on the latest chemicals and on the types of crops that were currently grown in the North, and the South Koreans were also well educated in this field.

On the day of their trip, the team loaded up in a van and headed to the border. At the border they were checked through then headed north to Pyongyang, picking up a military escort to the capital city. When they arrived in Pyongyang, they were met by military officers and civilians from their agriculture department. North Korea had planned several days of meetings, during which many different agricultural topics would be addressed. They planned a day of traveling to several local farms. During the field trips, the experts would meet with the farmers and examine the crops and soil.

The first several days in Pyongyang were productive as the team provided information on the latest farming techniques along with chemicals that would increase yields. The North Koreans were already doing some things that produced results, but the added information would make it better. There were simple things, like when and when not to water the crops, and more technical things associated with the newest chemicals and seeds.

The trips out to the farms were also productive. Looking at the crops and soils gave the team insight into how crops were growing. They could provide the assistance that would improve yield and quality.

The team had one last meeting in Pyongyang before traveling back to the South. In the meeting, they discussed how they would obtain the necessary seeds and chemicals, along with farming equipment. The team members said they would recommend to the officials in South Korea that they might possibly help in these areas. They were somewhat positive they could get these items from China, but South Korea helping would take cooperation to another level.

In Seoul, the officials in the South Korean government had discussions around helping North Korea with agriculture. The United Nations resolutions on North Korea were discussed in depth. The South Korean ambassador to the United Nations attended this meeting and provided input into what could and could not be done under the resolution. It was determined that the type of support they wanted to offer did not contradict the wording of the resolution, and South Korean officials decided they would help North Korea.

The South Koreans, using the communication system set up with the North, laid out the additional help they were going to offer in agriculture. The South Koreans also discussed the possibility of developing a more up-to-date communication system by installing cell towers in the North and the South to improve communications. Again, the North Korean officials said they would have to run it up the chain of command and would let them know as soon as a decision was made. The South Koreans thought they would probably agree with the agriculture proposal, but they were not sure on the cell tower communication proposal.

The answer from the North Korean officials came and was relayed to the officials in South Korea. The North Koreans said they would welcome help with agriculture, and they were still trying to decide if the countries should communicate by cell towers. The South Korean government turned to the three individuals who had traveled north and asked them to start putting together a list of items they needed, and the three of them got right to work developing the list. On the list were items such as seeds, chemicals, and equipment to help farmers. They also had visited one of North Korea's grain silos and made several suggestions to make them run smoother. The equipment and materials would be provided by South Korea, from South Korean companies.

To help with the materials and equipment, some of the largest companies in South Korea offered to help the government financially. The South Korean companies that produced the farm equipment provided the equipment at cost. With the government and the companies working together, they were able to gather a hundred million dollars of items the North needed. It was not hard to put together the help, considering the possibilities of the North and South further cooperating with each other.

It would take time to accumulate the equipment and materials, and during that time, there were several additional conversations between the two sides. One of the conversations involved better communication; specifically, the installation of two cell towers. The North Koreans, through conversations, had agreed to take the necessary steps to achieve this goal. Initially, the South Koreans suggested that the two towers should be set up between Pyongyang and Seoul, and the communication would be between the two countries' leaders. The North Koreans agreed with this suggestion. A timetable of installing the communication system was set for completion within the year.

The agricultural materials and equipment were sent to a large warehouse complex in South Korea. The trucks that were needed to haul these items were scheduled to run between the complex to a location inside North Korea. Many trips were made, and the total operation took several weeks to accomplish. There were no issues with the transport and delivery of equipment and materials. During the trips, both South Korean and North Korean officials traveled back and forth between the two sites. The operation was a complete success.

Both governments were also making progress with the new

communication system. As with the trip addressing agriculture, the South Koreans sent a team of experts to work on the communication tower and system in Pyongyang. While the team worked in Pyongyang, another team were also installing the system in Seoul. When installation was complete, they started the system, and the North could talk to the South. The communication system was online and functioning, and the two countries no longer communicated through the old system. To celebrate the new system, the leader of the North spoke to the leader of the South.

Officials from the North and South started to have conversations daily, discussing many topics. One of the main topics was the current sanctions imposed on them by the United Nations. South Korean representatives told the North Korean representatives they would start the process to possibly lift the sanctions. The first step the South Koreans needed to take was to contact the countries that had the most influence in the United Nations. With the two countries cooperating and great progress being made, South Korea had the power to influence the UN in putting it to a vote. There was a lot of work to be done to put together a package to submit to the UN and to distribute to other countries. The South Korean representatives contacted the North Korean representatives and asked them if they wanted to work together to create the documents to submit to the UN. The North Koreans were excited to be a part of putting together the documents and accepted.

For several months, the North and South Koreans worked together on the documents they needed to submit to the UN. When the documents were completed, the countries made a joint submission to the United Nations. The documents were also sent to the United States, China, Russia, and to Japan, Taiwan, China, Vietnam, Indonesia, and the Philippines. These Asian countries were interested in the documents because they hoped for a stable region. There were some concerns brought up by some of the countries, but the overall feeling was that a united Korea would be good for them and the entire region. The support from the Asian countries would only help both Koreas with the UN.

Chapter 16

Sanctions Lifted

The process to have the sanctions removed was similar to the process to have the sanctions approved. The United States was not involved in the process because both Koreas were submitting the proper documents and then getting the resolution through the process. The ambassadors of both North and South Korea were working together in this process. There was a good feeling that the sanctions would be lifted because of the backing by the other Asian countries. The United States officials did not think the sanctions should be lifted, but representatives were open to further discussion.

Both North and South Korea wanted to have the support of the United States, so they set up a meeting in New York at the UN headquarters. The United States ambassador was present in the meeting with the ambassadors of South and North Korea. In the meeting they discussed many topics, and specifically talked about the work the two countries had been doing in agriculture and communications. The US ambassador was happy that the two Koreas were working together but was concerned about the nuclear ambitions of North Korea. The primary reason the sanctions had been imposed was to try to get the North Koreans to stop developing nuclear weapons.

"Miss Ambassador, we are not working on nuclear weapons for war.

We only want to keep the rest of world from shutting us out," said the North Korean ambassador.

"This is completely different from what my government thought were the reasons," she said.

"We want to be recognized as a country, the same as Japan or South Korea," he said.

"If this is your intent, then some things must to be done by your country before you will have the support of the United States."

"I realize that words are words and actions speak louder than words. I want to also add that we are exploring the use of nuclear materials to provide power to the country. You cannot find a power generation source as clean as nuclear energy, with the exception of wind or water. Please take this information to Washington," he said.

"I'll discuss this with them. Thanks for your time," she said.

The US ambassador was on the phone to Washington minutes after the meeting. She talked to the secretary of state about her meetings with North and South Korean representatives. She talked about every detail, from what was taking place in the North and the South, and the North's nuclear program. Her initial feeling about the meeting was that it was productive. They had made some good points to be considered.

"This is a fight that will go nowhere," said the secretary of state. "We have had a terrible relationship with North Korea for so many years that most politicians are not willing to discuss lifting sanctions," he added.

"I realize that, Mr. Secretary, but would you please try to get a response from the president?" she said.

"I'll talk to him about this matter and let you know." The secretary ended the call and quickly picked up the phone to talk to the assistant secretary of state.

The meeting with the president at the White House was held a week after the phone conversation with the president and several members of Congress. The secretary of state had his staff put together a small package of information. "Mr. President, the information in front of you is a detailed summary of our conversation with the North Korean ambassador," he said.

"You are aware of the stance of the administration to not support any resolution that would lift the sanctions," he replied.

"I'm aware, sir, but I wanted to highlight a few things. The first is the complete change in our interpretation of why they were constructing the nuclear arsenal. The second is their research into nuclear power generation," he said.

"I see that, but again, because they have said nothing about stopping their nuclear program, these are just words," said the president. "I have to give them points for stopping the underground nuclear testing," he added. "Call the US ambassador and tell her the position of this government is to not support the resolution at the UN to remove the sanctions."

"Yes, sir," he said. The secretary of state informed the US ambassador to the UN of their decision. The word of the United States' stance on lifting the sanctions was relayed to the North and South Korean ambassadors. They were both disappointed but were not surprised.

Both Koreas had been working on the other nations that had influence because they were the larger countries. They had given the same presentation at meetings with Russia and China, also with Germany, France, and the United Kingdom. They had the Asian countries on board, China being one of them. It was a little harder persuading the European countries. They knew that, with the United States against it, the United Kingdom would fall in line and vote against. France and Germany were more open, especially with the North wanting to eventually use nuclear material for power generation. They also knew they had said this was a possible use of the nuclear material, and it was a fact, not a lie to get the sanctions lifted. They had left the meeting with the European countries with the feeling that they might back the resolution. They did not get a simple yes or no, and they would not know until the vote was taken.

During the days leading up to the resolution, meetings were scheduled with even more UN countries. These might not be the larger countries, but they had votes like everyone else. Countries such as Brazil, Argentina, Australia, Canada, and Spain were involved in these meetings. The United States, and probably the United Kingdom, were sure to vote no, and the Asian countries would vote yes. But there were some good feelings about some of the remaining countries. It was possible that the resolution would pass and the sanctions would be lifted.

As it had been with the previous resolution to impose sanctions, the UN would hear the resolution and then return in a week for the official vote. On the day of the resolution, representatives from both South and North Korea took turns at the podium and addressed the nations. After the presentations were finished, the UN nations were asked to provide any questions to the North and South ambassadors. The United States ambassador stood at the podium and laid out the United States' case to keep the sanctions on North Korea. No other country would talk in front of the UN assembly after the US spoke. Most of the larger countries had already talked to the Korean ambassadors from both the North and the South, so there were few questions from the other nations. The UN meeting ended with a vote scheduled for the following week.

In the week running up to the vote, both North and South Korea answered some of the questions from the smaller nations. Representatives held meetings with as many countries as they could during the week. Most of the questions were centered around the nuclear ambitions of the North, and they addressed the questions the same as before. By now, they were getting a better feeling as to whether the resolution would pass or not.

On the day of the vote, the UN secretary gave a small speech about the resolution, and then the assembly voted. The resolution to lift sanctions on North Korea passed. Delegations from North and South Korea, along with delegations from other countries in Asia, expressed approval of the outcome. They were on their phones calling to let the leaders and officials with their governments know how the vote went and which countries voted for or against the resolution.

Tom was notified of the vote through John. At this point in the relationship between the two Koreas, Tom thought things would start speeding up between them. It was the beginning of the year, and with regard to the Ring of Fire earthquake activity, there had been no larger earthquakes like the previous one.

After the vote, there were celebrations in the capital cities of both North and South Korea. There was also a joint celebration located close to the border crossing. At the joint celebration, the leaders from the North and the South spoke to the crowd of South Koreans and North Koreans. People from other countries, such as Japan, Taiwan, China, and the Philippines, were also in attendance and took part in the celebration. Both Tom and Rachel were invited to attend the celebration, along with John.

During the speeches, it was brought up that the North and South would be building another access between the two countries. Officials from both countries had been having daily conversations using the new communication system, and all agreed that another access point between the countries would be helpful in the future. The location was determined to be not far from the existing crossing. Both sides would still have a military presence at the borders, but the hope was that this would not be the case in the future. The entire project would last over a year and would involve construction personnel from both sides.

For the first time in many years, the general population of both countries had good feelings about future possibilities. The relationship between the Koreas was the main topic discussed by many South Koreans. People talked about it at work and even in the streets.

John called Tom to relay thanks from the South Korean government.

"Tom, I wanted to let you know that the South Korean ambassador called me the other day."

"Hope it is not something bad," he replied.

"No, he wanted to thank you for the work you've been doing monitoring the Ring of Fire and specifically for obtaining the data from North Korea."

"I was never going to give up trying to retrieve the canister," said Tom.

"Without using that data in the first place to get a resolution passed, all of the cooperation between North and South never would have happened."

"I appreciate the thank you. Please relay that to the ambassador."

"I'll talk to you soon," said John.

At Tom's office, staff members talked about the possibilities. "I think this cooperation might lead to opening the borders," said Tom.

"The North is certainly going to need to work on the infrastructure of the country," replied Mark.

"If the borders are open, it will take years to build infrastructure," said Rachel.

"At least, you won't get arrested like I did for crossing into the country," said Tom. All three of them, along with several other staff members, started to laugh.

John had sent pictures to Tom of the area already being cleared for the new access point between the countries. He also wrote in his email that the construction phase would be starting soon. The next step was to open all borders between the two countries and set up a system like other countries had in place for passing between the borders. There were not many entry points between the two countries, so the process could start small and then grow with the construction of more crossings.

Chapter 17

Border between South Korea and North Korea Opened

At the office in Seoul, Tom was reading an email on the progress between the North and South. As the late summer moved into fall, both all borders were opened for travel between the two countries. In the beginning, they would allow only traffic between North and South Korea and China, but eventually they opened them up for the Asia, countries, and then finally opened them for the rest of the world. South Koreans entering North Korea and North Koreans entering South Korea had to show identification—a passport or driver's license—that proved their citizenship.

Once the border was open, Tom sent word to Kim in North Korea letting her know that he and Rachel were going to take a trip to see the country and stop by her office. Tom set a date to meet with Kim.

Tom could tell by reading emails that many people from the South were traveling to the North, but they would spend only a day because there were not enough places to stay such as hotels. He had set up his visit with Kim at the last minute, so Tom could not find any rooms to stay in when traveling to the North. Rachel had walked into his office. "Just sent word to Kim about us traveling to see North Korea and visiting with her," he said.

"So, she was okay with us visiting her?" she replied.

"Yes, she sounded excited about meeting and showing us her office. There is one problem, though. We're going to have to find a place and sleep in a tent," said Tom.

"I don't have any problem with camping. I camped several times growing up," she said.

The process of building more hotels and places to stay in North Korea would take years, and the government had started with that plan as soon as the border was opened. In addition to rooms, the country would need restaurants and improvements to infrastructure such as roads and bridges. There were restaurants in the country, and they were busy constantly now that the people from the South were visiting. The money spent in the North would boost the country's economy.

Over the last several months of the year, the leaders of the two countries held high-level talks to discuss the progress and the upcoming Winter Olympics in Seoul. Both leaders were happy with the progress between the Koreas. There would be plenty more work to do, and this work would take years to accomplish, but both countries were moving ahead with 100 percent cooperation.

When the day arrived for Tom and Rachel to travel North, Tom picked up Rachel at her house at around eight in the morning. "Buckle up, Rachel," he said. "We have many hours of driving before we arrive in Pyongyang." he said.

"Don't speed up there. We should arrive with plenty of time before it gets dark," she said.

When they arrived outside the capital city, Tom found a spot where other South Koreans had stopped and set up a camping area. There were some larger recreation vehicles but mostly tents with open fires. "I'll set up the tent, Rachel, if you can get the camping items and the cooler," he said."

"I'll grab those items and start a fire for us to cook over," she said.

When they were settled, they sat around the fire and talked. "Was this what it was like when you were on your mission in North Korea?" she asked.

"Yes, but a little different. We couldn't start a fire because of the chance someone would see it," he said. "What are your thoughts about meeting Kim in the morning at her office?" he said.

"I want to see how the monitors that Jeff set up are working and what her office looks like," she replied.

"I would also like to see the setup," said Tom. When it was time to sleep, Tom crawled into the tent and then Rachel did the same. Tom thought this was the closest he had ever slept next to Rachel. He started to feel excitement that they were sleeping next to each other. His feelings of love for Rachel had only increased. He fell asleep with a picture in his head of he and Rachel getting married.

In the morning, they arrived at Kim's office, and she greeted them outside the building. "It is great to see you again, Tom," she said.

"Good to see you also, Kim," he replied.

Kim reached her hand out to Rachel. "How are you doing, Rachel?" Kim said.

"I'm doing fine."

The three of them walked into the building and up to the floor where Kim's offices were located. They were given a tour of the offices and met several of Kim's staff members. When they completed the tour, Kim invited them to dinner at her home. She gave Tom the address and directions before Tom and Rachel left the office.

For the rest of the day, Tom and Rachel drove around Pyongyang and stopped at several sites. When it was getting close to the time they had agreed to meet at Kim's, Tom followed the directions, and they arrived at her home. Tom looked around for a door bell but couldn't find one, so he knocked on her door. Kim opened the door and showed them to the living room. The furniture that was upholstered in fabric, and the picture on the wall was of the city of Pyongyang. "Nice place you have here, Kim," said Tom.

"I've been living here for about five years now," she said. "I just finished cooking, and it is ready to eat." She put a dish on the table. Tom and Rachel walked into the dining area and sat down. "I have cooked a traditional North Korean dish for dinner," she said.

"It smells delicious," said Rachel. At dinner they talked about the opened borders and the future of both Koreas. When it was time for them to leave, Tom made a comment that caught Kim's attention. "Well, Rachel, I guess we have to go set up the tent again," he said.

"At least we had a wonderful dinner and don't have to worry about cooking," she said.

"I don't want your first experience in North Korea to be camping out in a tent," said Kim. "I have a spare room with a bed, and you are welcome to sleep there tonight," she added.

"Thank you for offering the spare room for us," said Tom. Tom and Rachel brought in their overnight bags. "I can sleep on the floor, Rachel," said Tom.

"No, you don't have to do that. The bed is large enough for both of us," she said. As Tom fell asleep again close to Rachel for the second night, he was thinking about her. He thought about sleeping last night in the tent, and this night sleeping in a bed. *This is what a married couple would be doing*, he thought.

The next morning, Tom and Rachel got up and ready, then thanked Kim for letting them stay at her home. "If you are ever in South Korea, please look me up," said Tom. "You don't have to book a hotel room because you can stay at my house," he added.

"Thanks, Tom, I'll keep that in mind," said Kim. Tom and Rachel started their drive back to South Korea. They stopped in a small town in southern North Korea to take a break and look around the town. There were no tall buildings, only one- and two-story buildings. There were vehicles, but not as many as they would see in South Korea.

They stopped to talk to one of the residents in the town. They asked him who he was and what he did for a living. He said that his name was

Lee and he worked in the local metal shop in town. Tom asked him if he had a family, and he said he did. Tom was interested in whether there was adequate food to take care of his family. Lee said his family did have food but not an abundance, only the minimum. Lee was grateful to have enough food for his family, and many families also had enough food. Rachel asked Lee what type of metal work he worked on, and he said he made small items such as chimes and bottle openers. She asked him if she could purchase one of the chimes. They walked several blocks to his metal shop where Rachel picked out what she liked and paid Lee for the chimes.

Tom and Rachel got into their vehicle and drove off toward the border. At the border there was a fifteen-minute wait to cross because of all the traffic, but the experience was smooth and without any problems. There were cars, trucks, and recreational vehicles at the border. They arrived back in Seoul at around six in the evening, and Tom took Rachel to her home. Both of them got out of the vehicle, and Tom helped unload her bags. "Well, I had a great time," he said.

"I did also," she replied.

"I look forward to seeing you at the office," said Tom. For a split second, Tom acted out of impulse and hugged Rachel.

She was surprised, and instantly started to have romantic feelings for Tom. While Tom drove away from Rachel's home, he was picturing the two of them arriving at their home.

The open border was working well between the two Koreas, and the border between China and North Korea was working well also. With the use of passports, officials were able to determine if people were from South Korea or China. Discussions turned to increasing the trade between the countries; specifically, installing a rail line between the North and

South so the South could send bulk shipments of materials and equipment. There were existing rail lines in South Korea close to the border, and the closest rail line was over a hundred miles inside North Korea, so there needed to be engineering and route layout before construction could begin on the rail line. Work would start on this project in the middle of year, and talks were needed with the main railroad companies in South Korea, along with those in North Korea.

The next day, after Tom arrived in Seoul, he stopped by his bank in the morning before work to exchange the money he had left over from their trip to North Korea. At the office, he had a call with Kyle in Washington. The conversation revolved around his trip to North Korea and the meeting with Kim Yong-Suk. Tom briefed Kyle on their work with the North Koreans and discussed what he had seen of the progress since the borders had opened.

Kyle informed Tom there were a lot of upset people in Washington after the resolution had passed. From congressmen to the president, they continued to think that North Korea should have been forced to stop their nuclear ambitions before any sanctions were lifted. Some of them were upset with the open borders and the cooperation between the governments. Tom added what he had seen—things were running fine, and this would be a great thing for both North Korea, South Korea, and all of Asia.

During this activity with the opening borders and the work being developed, there were some problems in the beginning. But officials from both Koreas would work together to resolve the issues in a professional manner. For example, in the beginning, soldiers from both the North and the South were taking too long and making it hard for visitors to pass through the border. This issue was addressed within days, and the result was a better border crossing.

During this year of change, there was not much information on the status of the North's nuclear program. There were no more underground tests, but the status of the program was still unknown. During their conversations, the two leaders spoke about the North's nuclear program only once, and there was not much said about it. The officials from the North did reiterate that the underground testing was finished. Officials from the South knew they had been trying to develop missiles, but nothing more. The South Korean officials chose not to push the issue with the North; instead, they took a different approach and spoke gradually about the issue.

At the same time officials from South Korea were talking with officials from North Korea, the officials from the South had been having talks with China on the same issue. China had always had a military influence in some matters with North Korea, and the South Korean officials thought they could help. China was initially reluctant to dive into this area and wanted to drag the process out. Given the current situation with borders open and things moving at a rapid pace, South Korean officials pressed China to get involved. Chinese officials agreed to talk to the North Koreans about their nuclear plans and would leave their conversation with South Korea out of the conversation.

Chinese diplomats held talks with the North Korean officials and with their leader. The point they wanted the North to think about was the status of their country with South Korea and China. The open borders and the cooperation should include the removal of the nuclear arms issue. There was no need to keep working on these arms, and especially a missile system. If North Korea kept on this path, many people would not want to travel to their country, especially from South Korea and China. This was not a guess, but a fact, and they told the North that, in a poll they had taken in China and South Korea, the majority had fallen in line with their point. The conversations were productive, and the officials from China felt that the North Koreans might stop, but they would need further conversations.

The North Koreans held their own meetings to discuss the status of their nuclear program and to discuss the meetings with Chinese and South Korean representatives. The border opening and trade taking place between the Koreas and China was helping their economy. Things were going fine with the South and China, and they knew that to increase the economy more, they needed to stop the development of nuclear weapons. They also addressed the conversations that took place with other nations during the vote of the United Nations.

Tom arrived at the office in Seoul, but this day was different from most. Kim Yong-Suk, from North Korea was scheduled to arrive at the office that morning. She was coming to his office to look at the entire system they monitored, just as Tom and Rachel had visited her office.

When she arrived, Tom met her in the main computer room. Soon, Rachel walked into the room. Tom had planned to show Kim around the room and then meet in the conference room to talk. He took her on the tour showing her the television monitors and explaining what the computers did and how they worked together for the people's safety around the Ring of Fire.

"This is impressive. There are several items you have that I wish I had at my office," said Kim.

"Who knows, Kim? With the relations between the two Koreas, you might be able to get those items for your office," replied Tom. The offer stands for dinner at my house, and also you can stay there," he said.

"I'll definitely have dinner with you, but I have made arrangements to stay at a hotel," she said.

"Let's say seven o'clock at my house," said Tom. Kim wanted to shop in Seoul, so she left the office.

Later in the evening, Kim arrived at Tom's house. Rachel was already there helping Tom with dinner. They fixed Kim a traditional South Korean dinner so she could get a feel for the food in South Korea. "What would you like to drink, Kim?" said Tom.

"I'll have a glass of wine," she replied. "Rachel, are you going to drink wine also?"

"Yes, please pour me a glass," she said. Tom took the two glasses of wine to Kim and Rachel.

At the dinner table, the discussion turned to the upcoming Olympics in South Korea. "Will you be attending the Olympics, Kim?" asked Tom.

"I can't afford to attend the Olympics, but I'd really like to see some of the events," she said. "The television stations in North Korea don't carry the winter games," she added.

"That might change someday also," said Tom.

"You might have satellite television with over one hundred channels," said Rachel.

"I don't know what I would do if I could watch one hundred different channels. It would certainly make my evenings more pleasant," said Kim.

When it was time for Kim to leave, she thanked Tom and Rachel and left Tom's house around ten.

In the morning, Tom and Rachel met with Kim for coffee before heading to the office. Kim had a little more shopping to do before she traveled back to Pyongyang. Tom and Rachel headed to the office. At the office, they checked in with Mark to get an update, and Mark informed Tom there had been a malfunction with one of the monitors in Taiwan. Tom would normally head to the monitor to make repairs, but this time he asked Mark to travel and repair the monitor.

For many years, Tom and Rachel had a working relationship traveling to many parts of Asia, working on monitors, and attending conferences. They were the best of friends and had shared many happy—as well as sad—moments. With Tom's feelings of love for Rachel growing stronger, he thought it was getting close to the time when he should let her know. He did not know if it was because he was not getting any younger, or whether living by himself for all these years made him want to have a partner to spend time with. He had no idea how Rachel felt about him. Maybe she just thought about him as a work partners and best friend. He thought she might not be interested, or maybe it would even get to the point where she did not want to work with him and would transfer somewhere if he pursued it further. He loved her as a friend and as a person, and he wanted to let her know his feelings.

There was no way for him to know how she felt other than to talk to her about his feelings. He decided the best way would be to invite her to dinner at one of his favorite restaurants in Seoul. After running over possible scenarios many times in his head, he got the nerve up to ask her to dinner.

She was thinking this would be like the many dinners in the past, and they would discuss earthquakes and tsunamis during dinner. She did have a thought, however, that this dinner might be a little different from the dinners they'd had in the past. She had picked up on Tom's nervousness when he invited her to dinner and could tell by his tone of voice that something was different.

On the night of their dinner date, Tom arrived at the restaurant a little early to get a table that was private and not in the middle of the floor. The tables were made of wood, and the chairs were metal with soft brown cushions. There was a glowing candle on each table, and the walls were covered with pictures of romantic sites. Rachel walked into the restaurant, and when she looked at Tom, her suspicions were even stronger. Tom met her at the table, and they both sat down. The waiter came to the table. Tom ordered a beer, while Rachel ordered wine.

Tom was nervous, so he decided to talk about work with her first.

"There hasn't been any activity around the Ring of Fire, which is a good thing," he said.

"It is a good thing," replied Rachel. "Everything is up and functioning, so if something did occur, we would know about it," she added.

After they discussed Kim Yong-Suk's visit to Seoul, Tom had the perfect opportunity to tell her his feelings. "Rachel, I know we have had a great working professional relationship, but I can't stop the romantic feelings I have for you," he said. "I have fallen in love with you."

Rachel responded in only a few seconds, but it seemed like an hour to Tom. "Over the past few months, I have started to have romantic feelings about you," she said. "I have been trying to figure out a way to let you know my feelings, Tom."

Tom was relieved that she felt the same about him because he had been unsure how things would turn out. "What cities around the world would you like to visit?" asked Tom.

"I have always wanted to visit London," said Rachel.

"I have wanted to visit Rome," replied Tom. "What is your favorite recreation sport?"

"I like to ski," she said. "How about you?"

"I also like to ski." When they finished dinner and talking they left the restaurant and walked out to their vehicles. Tom turned to Rachel and gave her a kiss. Once this happened, he could feel the spark, and she felt the same thing. They both got into their vehicles and headed to their homes.

Chapter 18

Olympics in South Korea

During the first months of the year, many people in South Korea were busy. The Winter Olympics were to begin in February, and there was plenty of work to be done taking care of the venues and increasing labor for the influx of people. To help the South, North Korea sent a delegation of people. The North Koreans were planning to send athletes to compete in the Olympics. Some past Olympic athletes from North Korea were picked to run with the Olympic torch as it made its way through South Korea.

Before he started to date Rachel, Tom had made sure he was able to get tickets to the Olympic venues so they could attend together. He also had tickets to the opening ceremonies and had booked rooms close to the venues. Now that they were dating, the Olympic events would be a lot more exciting for them both. Tom spent the weeks leading up to the event at the office and going on dates with Rachel to places around Seoul.

The day before the opening ceremonies, Tom and Rachel drove into the city and checked into the hotel. There was a lot of traffic on the way to the ceremonies. The drive took an hour and a half longer because of the traffic. There were many people walking around the area where they were staying because there were lots of places to shop and eat.

There were people from countries from all around the world, and Tom and Rachel met a couple from the United Kingdom. The couple had made it to the last five Olympic winter games. They had arrived a few days earlier and were impressed with the shops and restaurants. After speaking with them for about fifteen minutes, Tom and Rachel headed to the trolleys and traveled to the area where the downhill skiing would take place. "It sure would be fun to ski on these slopes," said Tom.

"We might get the opportunity after the Olympics," replied Rachel.

"The ski slopes will be available after the games," he said.

They traveled back to their rooms at the hotel, and Tom kissed Rachel before walking to his room next door. The next day, the opening ceremonies would take place, so they both wanted to get rested for the event.

On the morning of the opening ceremonies, Tom and Rachel had a good breakfast at the hotel. While they ate, they put a small schedule together. They wanted to leave for the opening ceremonies in time get there and get seated. The event was going to start at eight that evening, so they made plans to leave the hotel around five. The trolley ride would be about thirty minutes with the traffic. When they got off the trolley, they would spend the next thirty minutes checking through the gates and getting to their seats.

The opening ceremonies started promptly at eight o'clock. In the beginning, there was a speech from the leader of South Korea and a speech from the head of the Olympic Committee. What happened next was a surprise to Tom and Rachel, and everyone else in the stadium. The leader of North Korea stood at the podium and started to talk. "I want to speak briefly about the cooperation between North Korea and South Korea. Now that the borders are open and trade is taking place between our two countries, there is no more need to further our nuclear program. Starting tonight, North Korea will cease all nuclear operations and dismantle our weapons. I wanted to say these things at this event because the Olympics show what you can achieve when you cooperate," he said. As he walked away from the podium, the attendees in the stadium erupted in applause.

Both Tom and Rachel were shocked after hearing the speech. This was something they thought they would never hear from the leader of North Korea. "What do you think this will lead to?" said Tom.

"I think it will lead to peace around the region," she said.

"The main issue has always been North Korea's nuclear program. Remove that threat, and peace will take place," he said.

On the way back to the hotel, Tom overheard people in the trolley talking about the speech. It was the number-one topic people were talking about; the actual ceremony was secondary. During the entire trolley ride, Tom could hear people talking about it.

When they finally got to their hotel, Rachel sat with Tom in his room, and they watched the television, which was buzzing about the speech. It seemed that every channel was covering the event. Most of what they were saying on the news was positive, reflecting the general attitude of the two Koreas. After a few hours of watching TV and talking to each other, Rachel returned to her room.

For the next several days, Tom and Rachel traveled to the venues and watched the competition—downhill skiing, bobsledding, and figure skating. In between events, they spent some quality time just being with each other kissing and being in love. On their final night at the hotel, they enjoyed a romantic dinner, and Rachel stayed in Tom's room for the rest of the night. They watched some television and drank wine before getting to the part both wanted to get to.

They arrived back in Seoul on a Friday afternoon, so the weekend was approaching. "Would you like to stay with me at my home this weekend, Rachel?"

"Yes, I would love to stay with you," she replied.

"I'll drop you off at your house, and then you can drive to my house," he said.

"Give me about two hours, and I'll be at your house."

After leaving Rachel's house, Tom went to the grocery store to pick up some items. He wanted to cook spaghetti and meatballs for her. He also picked up several bottles of wine. They had a wonderful evening together eating, drinking, and talking. During the weekend, they decided they were going to book a trip to Colorado to go skiing, so they ordered their tickets and reserved the hotel room. At work on Monday, they would put in for the time off.

After the closing ceremony of the Olympics, all the accounts on the news called it a successful Olympics for South Korea. The television reports indicated that all the venues had been attended by many people. It was too early to tell if it was a financial success, but all indications were that it would turn out to be profitable. As it had been in the winter Olympics of the past, countries such as the Finland, Norway, and Germany had the highest medal count.

Many things were running smoothly between the two Koreas. The borders were open, and people were traveling to both countries. Construction work was taking place in North Korea, and many other plans were just getting started. Farmers were starting to reap better crops, a direct result of the agricultural material and equipment they had received. Both countries were moving along at a fast pace.

It had been over a year since North Korea announced it had stopped underground testing. At Tom's office, everything was fine. One area Tom thought they were lacking in was monitoring inland and off the coasts of Burma, Thailand, and Malaysia. With the additional money in his budget, he put together three teams, one to travel to each of these countries. He allotted one week for each team to install two inland monitors and one buoy monitor.

The teams all left on a Monday and would return on Friday. Tom's team traveled to Malaysia to install the monitors. Mark's team traveled to Burma, and Rachel's team traveled to Thailand. Tom had preplanned the locations to install the monitors and had received approval from the countries. On Monday morning, all three teams departed, carrying their computers, while the monitors had been shipped to the capitals of the countries.

Tom and his team traveled to Kuala Lumpur, and after landing, picked up the rental van and drove to one of the monitor locations. They had decided to install one of the monitors in the downtown area of the capital. The other would be installed near the Bombalai volcano, and the buoy monitor would be installed in the ocean in the northeast part of the country that faces Japan and the other buoy monitors.

Rachel's team arrived in Bangkok and headed with the monitors to a location in the city of Bangkok and then to the volcano Phanom Rung. The buoy monitor would be installed in the Indian Ocean off the coast of the country. They chose a location in the ocean off the southern part of Thailand, in the boot. Because of the preplanning, the installation of the monitors went smoothly without any problems.

Mark's team arrived in Myanmar and installed one of the monitors in the city. They traveled to the lower Chindwin volcano and installed a monitor at that location. Finally, they installed the buoy monitor in the Indian Ocean off the coast of the country. There was a problem with one of the monitors because it would not communicate with Mark's laptop. Luckily, he had a spare part in his bag that he installed to get it working again.

None of the three volcanoes in which they installed monitors was considered active; they had all been dormant for many years. It was still the logical place to install devices because volcanoes are links to the underground plates many feet below the ground.

The three teams returned to Seoul on Friday afternoon at various times, and they were all going to meet in the conference room at the office first thing Monday morning.

On Monday morning in the conference room, each team leader was present to talk about the installations. Tom started the conversation, going through what he and his team had done in Malaysia. In the conference room there was a large-screen television that was tied to the other monitors in the office area. Tom pulled up the map of Malaysia. The two inland locations and one ocean location showed up on the screen as stars. They could zoom in on the locations. The map was as clear as a Google Earth image. Tom pointed out the proximity of the monitor to the volcano. The buoy monitor showed up on the map, and its location in relation to the monitors in the Philippines and Japan was clear. He talked about the installation process and said there had been no issues.

Both Rachel and Mark spoke about the countries where they had installed monitors, and Mark spoke some about the issue he had with the monitor he had to fix with the spare part. After they talked about the installations, the three of them spent about an hour pulling up the other monitors on the screen. There was only small activity taking place in the form of tremors. Looking at the entire system again gave Tom confidence they had most of the region covered.

The remainder of the year, Tom spent in Seoul working at the office and spending as much time as he could with Rachel. By the end of the year, Rachel had moved in with Tom and had sold her home. They took their vacation skiing in Colorado for a week, but it was the only time the two of them were not working. They both took a work trip to a conference during the year, but they did not need to speak at the conference.

The work to help North Korea continued, and by the end of year there were many more hotels in North Korea, and a new border crossing was close to being finished. The border with China was progressing with new roads and bridges. The residents of both North and South Korea were happy with the progress made.

Chapter 19

People of North Korea Pull Out of Poverty

In the beginning of new year, the traffic between the two Koreas and China had increased, almost doubling the number of Chinese and South Korean visitors. There had been little problem between the two countries, and construction continued at a rapid pace. By now there were signs that the economy in North Korea had strengthened, and many small businesses were starting in the country. These businesses were concentrated mainly in the capital, but there were also new businesses in cities along the main road from the border to Pyongyang.

North Korean farmers had been able to improve both quality and yield in main areas where rice and potatoes were farmed. They were producing enough produce to be easily able to feed the country and export extra to South Korea and China. With help from China and South Korea, the North planned to start growing fruit products to be used and sold by their people.

One only needed to drive in downtown Pyongyang to notice that there were more new cars being driven by North Korean people. The people were starting to pull out of a state of poverty and look ahead at their possibilities. South Korea's economy had gotten a boost from the open borders. Their main manufacturers of products like cars and construction equipment had ramped up production and now even had backlogs.

These manufacturers had been hiring new workers to meet the demand for everything from backhoes to skid loaders.

The lifting of the sanctions increased the traffic at the main piers in North Korea. Ships loaded with oil were showing up daily. The oil was quickly unloaded and trucked inland. Materials for construction were shipped to these piers from other Asian countries. The two Koreas were working out the details to build banks in North Korea to handle the influx of money.

At the office, Tom was working on calculations for one of the computer inputs when the alarm was activated, indicating seismic activity. There had been an earthquake out in the ocean off the southern coast of Japan, close to the buoy monitor they had installed. The readings they received showed a 5.2 on the Richter scale, and it was 1.2 miles deep. Tom got on the phone with the Japanese officials to confirm that they had also received the alarm. He also contacted the officials in the Philippines and in Taiwan. All three countries had received the alarm. Because of the size of the earthquake, there would be a small wave that would arrive on the shores of some of the countries. Calculating the earthquake size and depth, the computer indicated the wave would be close to two and a half feet high when it came to shore.

The wave was large enough to cause officials to activate the tsunami sirens on the coasts of Japan, Taiwan, South Korea, and the Philippines. They wanted to make sure people were aware of a wave coming, and even though it was not tall at two and a half feet, it still could knock somebody down if they were on the shore. The sirens worked the way they were designed, and people along the shores started to head inland and get to a higher elevation.

Tom and his team could not physically be there in time for the wave to arrive, so he relied on the officials in each country to calculate the wave height and then send the information to him. It would take some time before the wave reached the shores and then more time to calculate its height, so Tom would not get this information for several days. Tom spent this time analyzing the additional data the computer system had determined. This quake had occurred within ten miles of the buoy monitor, and it was the first time that a sizable earthquake had occurred within a close distance to a monitor.

Tom finally received the information on the wave. As predicted, the height had averaged approximately two and a half feet. He gave this information to Mark so he and the team could input the data into the computer program. With the data entered into the program, Tom watched as the computer did not make any changes to the locations and the probability. There were also no new locations that the program considered to be potential earthquake locations. Tom sent a team out to the buoy closest to the earthquake event to check it over.

A series of aftershocks occurred after this earthquake. They were small, ranging from 1.2 to a 3.4 on the Richter scale, and they did not affect the waves in any way. The aftershocks occurred in the same area as the earthquake had occurred, so there was no new location to put into the computer program.

Whenever there was an earthquake event, no matter how large, Tom would stop by a local bar to drink and think about the event. This time, he invited Rachel to have a drink at the bar. Since they were a couple now, Tom thought she should know what he did after an earthquake. "I always make it to a bar after an earthquake," he said.

"An earthquake and tsunami can rattle anyone," she said. I'm going to have a drink also, Tom."

"I hope there is never a large earthquake and tsunami," Tom said. "No matter how fast the tsunami sirens activate, there are always people that ignore the warnings. There is a lot of comfort knowing the computer system will perform well and sound the alarms. If it occurred like the recent earthquake many miles away in the ocean, the local authorities would have time to try to clear the shores. If it was a lot closer, there would only be the sirens sounding," he said.

"You can do only the best you can do," she said. "If people ignore the sirens, then they take responsibility for themselves."

As they drove to Tom's house, they both were hoping a large earthquake and tsunami would never occur so there would be no loss of life. Tom had had many drinks that night, so Rachel drove the vehicle.

When they arrived at Tom's house, Tom staggered his way up the stairs and then straight to his bedroom where he fell onto the bed and was quickly asleep. Rachel took his clothes off and tucked him into bed. She would have another drink before she climbed into bed with Tom and fell asleep.

The next morning, Rachel had to shake Tom to wake him up. Tom needed to be at the office by eight o'clock for a conference call with Chung in China. Tom woke and took a quick shower before dressing and heading to the kitchen. He drank a cup of coffee and took a couple of pills for his headache.

By the time they arrived at the office, he did not have a headache, so Tom could think more clearly. He still wasn't finished with the hangover, but he could function well enough to have the conference call. During the call, they discussed the recent earthquake and the situation in China. An hour later, Tom ended the phone call with Chung.

The rest of the year was calm along the Ring of Fire. There were no large earthquake events, and the team performed their yearly checkup on the monitors. Everything was functioning correctly.

Tom and Rachel had been living to together for over a year, and their relationship kept getting stronger. Tom thought it was getting closer to the day when he would ask Rachel to marry him. He started to think about how he wanted to propose to her and where would be the most romantic location. He had been saving some money to purchase an engagement ring. He did not want the ring to be extravagant, but still wanted it to look terrific. He had managed to slip away from work for an hour or so to look at different types of rings. He had finally settled on a day and a location for the proposal.

Chapter 20

A Region in Peace

The start of the new year was the start of peace around Asia. The two Koreas and China were continuing with their work together. North Korean officials had opened the borders for the rest of the world to visit. A great many people from around the world wanted to visit the country. Many of the countries around Korea were trading with North Korea. The leader of North Korea had traveled to several places, such as Europe, China, and Russia, meeting leaders and opening more trade opportunities. On some of the trips, he traveled with the leader of South Korea. The development of the region was an example of what can be done if people work with each other.

There was no more talk of potential war between North and South Korea, only cooperation and peace. Many of the people in North Korea had raised their standard of living over the years. They could now afford items they never could have purchased in the past. Tom had planned to take another trip to North Korea to look at the progress. This would take place later in the year. He wanted to propose to Rachel before taking the trip.

Tom had decided on where he wanted to ask Rachel to marry him, and he had chosen the week. He would propose where they had stayed when they went to the Olympics, and it would happen next weekend. He had booked the same hotel room where they had stayed before. He had purchased the ring and had hidden it in his house. The week before, he had asked Rachel if she wanted to go skiing with him. The Olympic venue was open to the public now. She had been wanting to go skiing, and this location would be quite interesting because the Olympics had taken place there. They settled on leaving Friday morning and arriving before noon.

During the rest of the week leading up to Friday, Tom spent his time in meetings and on conference calls. He was in a great mood thinking of the weekend he and Rachel would spend together skiing. Tom had everything set for the weekend. He had booked a table at a restaurant near the hotel, and there he would ask her to marry him. He had even arranged for a bottle of champagne to be put into their hotel room while they were out at the restaurant.

On Friday morning, Tom fixed breakfast before they began their drive to the hotel. "I think I'm going to try the most difficult ski slope on this trip," he said.

"Don't break a leg doing it," Rachel said. "I'm going to ski on the medium-level slopes. I enjoy gliding down the mountain and not having to bump up and down over moguls!"

When they arrived at the hotel, they had several hours before the dinner that Tom had arranged. They went to the same stores they'd visited during the Olympics. They were planning on getting to the slopes mid-morning on Saturday. After returning from the shops, they took turns in the bathroom getting ready for dinner. Once they were ready to go to dinner, Tom slipped the ring into his pocket.

At the restaurant, they were seated at a corner table, again not in the center but in a more romantic, remote area. The lights in the restaurant were dim, and the small lights on the tables provided just enough light for the tables and the people sitting at them. Tom had thought he should get down on one knee and ask her to marry him before the food was served. After they received their drinks from the waiter, Tom stood up and then got down on one knee. "Rachel, will you marry me?"

"Yes, I'll marry you, Tom," she said. Tom slipped the ring on her finger and gave her a kiss. By now, other people sitting at nearby tables were watching the proposal take place. After she said yes and they kissed, several people in the restaurant started to clap.

For the rest of the dinner, they sat closer together and talked about when and where they would get married. On the walk back to the hotel, they held hands the entire time. In the room was the bottle of champagne that Tom had ordered. They toasted the engagement. "I love you so much, Rachel."

"I love you to." After they finished their drinks, they started kissing, which led to the lights being turned off in the room.

For all of the work Tom had done to expose the underground nuclear tests, he had been thanked only by the South Korean government. He was not the type to expect any thanks, because he was persistent and wanted change to happen. About a week after he and Rachel returned from their skiing trip, he answered the phone. "Tom, this is the secretary of state."

"Yes, sir, what can I do for you?"

"I'm calling you to personally to thank you for the work you did to help bring about peace in the region," he said.

"I was only doing my job, sir."

"This was well above just doing your job, Tom. Without your determination, the resolution would not have been developed and passed by the UN. The chain of events after it was passed set in motion the peace we see today." After the phone call Tom felt good.

Tom and Rachel were married in Seoul eight months from the time they got engaged. It was a small ceremony, attended by John, Mark, Martin, Kim Yong-Suk, and Chung. They honeymooned in Hawaii for a week before returning to Seoul.

Because of the success of the work Tom, Rachel, and their team, had done around the Ring of Fire, they began to travel to other parts of the world to give speeches on their system. Since their system was put online, similar systems were installed in other countries including South America and Europe. Tom and Rachel continue to work at the office in Seoul, monitoring the Ring of Fire.

About the Author

Wolf Blaser Jr. lives and works in Topeka, Kansas. *Disturbing the Ring of Fire* is his second book.